Why Kill An Angel?

C. Lee Tocci

Laurel Canyon Publishing
North Hollywood, California

This is a work of fiction.
Names, characters and incidents are either the product of the
author's imagination or are used fictitiously.
Any resemblance to actual persons, living or dead,
is entirely coincidental.

CHAPTER ONE

I now know why people confess to the police.

Anything is better than sitting there with everyone glaring at you and no one talking to you. You get to the point that you'd admit to killing Jimmy Hoffa just so someone will smile at you.

I felt like Hitler at a Bas Mitzvah.

I sat on the booking bench, my hands cuffed in front of me, charged with first degree murder and waited for my lawyer to arrive.

I bet you're wondering how a boring little real estate attorney like me could have possibly got into a mess like this.

Me too.

CHAPTER TWO

Two days. Forty eight hours. Isn't amazing how quickly your life can degenerate into absolute bedlam.

Monday afternoon. I pulled my car neatly into the only available spot on Bunker Hill, executing a perfect fourteen point parking maneuver, docking tightly against the curb, feeling quite pleased at having found a place only two and a half blocks away from my sister's condo.

As I walked towards her building, I could see the rush hour traffic that slogged along the Southeast Expressway. The sun glinted off the Boston skyline, blinding drivers and pedestrians alike as they headed home after having wasted a beautiful warm spring day at work.

At least those who showed up. New Englanders will find a way to get to work under the most catastrophic conditions, be it blizzards or political conventions or invasions from Yankee fans. They consider such obstacles a challenge and will plow through banks of snow and crowds of transients with a defiance worthy of their patriot predecessors.

Yet if the first warm day of spring happens to fall on a weekday, the most bizarre phenomenon of medical science occurs. Half of the clerical staff suddenly succumb to that chest cold that they have been fighting off all winter and call in sick.

Okay, so I exaggerate. It was only my admin assistant Rhonda that had called in sick that day. But it was an omen and I should have known that it was a bad start to what was going to be a very bad week.

As I stopped on the sidewalk outside my sister Julie's front door, I took a deep breath of Charlestown air.

Now Charlestown is only a couple of miles from downtown Boston, but for some reason, the air smells different. Yes, it smells of the sea, but somehow it smells brinier. Is that a word? It has the deep bitter tang of shipyards and lobster pots. It's a working class dock town and you can taste it in the air.

I kind of like it. It's reassuring and real. I took another deep breath, gathered my courage and entered the front door to the old brownstone.

CHAPTER THREE

You might ask why the sweet simmering smell of Veal Marsala would send my entire gastro-intestinal tract right up into my throat, but you don't know my sister. Julie was pulling out all the stops. This was not going to be a casual, insignificant dinner and when Julie went the distance, it was usually much farther than I, or the rest of the civilized world really wanted to go.

Let me explain: My sister is not just accident prone. She is not a mere magnet for disaster. She is a super-quasar black hole of chaos. From the time she could walk, calamity has followed in her wake. And not the normal, mortal skinned-knees/broken-arms /gashed-foreheads of childhood. Oh, no! She was actually kidnapped when she was four years old! When her kidnappers let her use the restroom at the Mobil station, the police moved in and there was a huge gun battle. By the time she came out, her kidnappers had been hauled off to the hospital and then to jail, and Julie was still wondering what the heck happened to the nice people that promised her an ice cream cone.

The problem is: Julie hasn't changed. She still believes everything that anyone tells her and truly thinks that all people are good and sweet and honest. And the reality is, Julie attracts all the people that are the polar extreme of good and sweet and honest.

At twenty-six, I am only eighteen months older than my sister, but I'm already going gray.

"Delicious!" I lied as I dived into the pie. Actually, it probably was delicious, but nothing during dinner had soothed my anxiety and by dessert, the angst had risen to my gut. The whole meal could have been cardboard and wallpaper paste for all I knew. All I could taste was dread. "So what did you want to tell me?"

Julie hesitated. I had a sudden deep regret that I didn't go to church this past Sunday. I didn't think that the cursory grace that we had sputtered through before dinner was enough compensation. I raced through a mental rosary. Years of practice and I've got the entire sequence down to under eight seconds.

It's one of my few gifts.

"Well, Jo, I have this great idea for a new business." Julie glowed as if she were giving me the keys to a new car. "Just you and me. It would be so great! What did you think?"

I waited. I said nothing. I waited. Julie beamed. She really has no clue.

"It's a Detective Agency. You know when we were kids and we wanted to be spies or detectives? Well I think we should just do it!"

I said nothing. I couldn't think of one word to

say. I said nothing.

"So what do you think?" She sat there like some hyper-puppy presenting me with a dead rat that she had just killed.

My mouth opened, but nothing came out. I flapped my lips once or twice to loosen up the cogs and swallowed hard. Then I looked her straight in the eye. There was only one answer to this question and there could be no room for wavering.

"No," I said decisively. "Absolutely not."

CHAPTER FOUR

Why can't she just accept "No" when I say "No"? She's been that way since we were kids.

This morning, against my better judgment, we were driving into Boston to keep an appointment that I knew perfectly well that we shouldn't be keeping.

Julie was singing along to an Alanis Morrisette CD that she had brought. She had a really sweet voice, not very strong, but pretty to listen to.

I sighed. Nothing I could say was going to change our course. Julie was too much like mama for mere logic to make any impression.

Our mother had died when we were kids and Dad had died two years ago when I was still in my last year of law school. So that just left me and Julie.

Dad had left Julie's half of his estate in trust for me to manage until she turned thirty. To anyone who didn't know us, this might seem strange, but Dad trusted me to take care of her and Julie knew I would manage it better than she could. Besides, she always could wheedle anything she wanted out of me.

I sighed again. I just hoped that I could keep strong on this one. I did not have a good feeling about this meeting.

I pulled off the expressway and was now weaving my way through the hodgepodge labyrinth of the North End of Boston.

I'm guessing there's no place else in North America that looks and feels more like old Europe than the North End of Boston. The streets are narrow and cobbled and weave around without rhyme or reason. Little old Italian men still walk the streets, talking with their hands. People still shop in corner markets and carry their groceries home every day. Cars park on the sidewalks and possibly the finest Italian restaurants on the planet are crammed between four story walk-up brownstones and ancient warehouses.

"Gentrification" has not passed the North End by. Upwardly mobile professionals have bought out and modernized much of the derelict buildings, but unlike most neighborhoods that have been assaulted by progress, the North End has absorbed the invaders and made them conform to its demands. You can wear Louis Vuitton suits instead of flowered housedresses, but you're still going to pick up a loaf of fresh bread, two pounds of vermicelli and a half pound of parmigiano cheese at the corner grocer.

And better to die an unconfessed sinner than even think about littering.

I pulled down a narrow alley off Salem Street and stopped in front of a five story graystone building with the number "64" elegantly painted on the glass transom over an antique carved door. At Julie's direction, I parked up on the sidewalk. Every instinct screamed against this. I was definitely a park-in-designated-spaces-and-obey-all-traffic-rules kind of person. I wouldn't last forty minutes in the North End.

From the sidewalk, five steps led down to a basement door. *Scollari and Sons, Private Investigators, est. 1962* read a sign that managed to look both modest and pretentious at the same time. I glanced up the street, half expecting to see a Studebaker careening down the alley with a tommy-gun-toting gangster spraying the storefronts with bullets. I felt like I had entered another dimension.

I wasn't going to last thirty minutes in the North End.

Julie grabbed my hand. "C'mon. We're a little late, but Teeny won't mind. He's cool."

"Teeny? His name is 'Teeny'?"

"Well, that's just what I call him. His name is really Tino."

As we walked down the steps, the gas bubble in my chest deflated a little. I can take a guy named Teeny.

Julie pushed open the door and we stepped inside. "Hey, Teeny! We're here!" Julie called out.

I heard some movement in the inner office and I took that moment to look around. I could see that someone had tried to straighten up, but there's only so much you can do with vintage flea market chic.

Evidently the room had been originally furnished by Dashiell Hammett and had only been redecorated once by Robert Parker. A lonely beam of sunlight struggled through a grimy basement window trying its best to help out a flickering antique ceiling light. The two desks in the outer office were 1940's era dark oak that had been chipped and dinged into submission. They no longer held any pretensions to being elegant: they were only utilitarian. The file cabinets that lined one wall were those old fashion grey aluminum horrors, two drawers were so banged up that they wouldn't shut, and I would have bet my Lexus that those were bullet holes that I saw along the front. Odd assortments of framed pictures and weird memorabilia lined the walls and shelves. Old black and white snapshots of men in suits shaking hands and smiling for the camera. Signed baseballs and vintage Red Sox caps. It even had a couple of shoulder holsters, complete with handguns, hanging on the coat rack.

I couldn't help but smile. It was everything that I expected and more. An Academy Award winning team of set designers couldn't have laid this out any better. I saw a shadow move against the frosted glass window on the door to the inner office and I held my breath, fully expecting Danny DeVito to walk through it at any moment.

The door opened. I'm not going to say that my first impression was disappointment, but I will tell you that it wasn't Danny DeVito.

"Jo, this is Teeny. Teeny... Jo." Julie had her proud puppy grin on as she glanced between us.

Teeny was not tiny. Teeny must have been at least six feet four inches tall and seemed near as much wide. Not that he was fat, he was just... vast. All he needed was a black helmet and a light saber and I would be face to face with Darth Vader. I flashed back to my high school mythology and I would have cast him as Vulcan, the god of fire and volcanoes, in a millisecond. His skin was dark and swarthy. His hair was dark brown, almost black, and curly. His eyes were dark too, under heavy dark brows. At first, I thought he had this uni-brow thing going, but it was just that his brows were knit together from glaring at me. He took a step towards me but I refused to step back. I held my ground and glared back up at him from my towering five foot four inch height.

My neck hurt. Blast, I wish I'd worn my four inch heels. I felt like a twelve year old standing between the pair of them.

"Joe? This your trustee, Joe?" His voice was rough with that North End-Revere accent that made you think of bodies stuffed in trunks and suspicious warehouse fires.

I took a deep breath. Okay then, let's get this over with.

"Not what you expected?" I asked, folding my arms in front of my chest.

He looked me up and down and his glare was replaced by a seemingly appreciative smile. I felt a slow burn coming on. It rarely bothered me that I wasn't as beautiful or as glamorous as Julie, but I really disliked his attitude in thinking that he could charm me out of my sister's money by ogling my legs. My hands moved to my hips and my chin came down. He met my glare with a smirk.

"I'm not disappointed, if that's what you're asking," he replied.

"Well, I am," I lied. "I was expecting Danny DeVito."

Tino shot an affectionate glance over at Julie. That surprised me. It wasn't the leer or the glare that I had received and it softened his whole face. I glanced between them, trying to read between the lines.

"Julie's the only human being that has ever called me 'Teeny'. Anyone else would be in the ICU at Mass General." He glanced back at me, the warm smile still on his face.

Uh oh, I thought, hang on to your checkbooks. This guy is good. He extended his hand and I found myself unintentionally placing my own in his. "You can call me Tino. Valentino Scollari."

"Jo. Josephine D'Angelo. You can call me... Ms. D'Angelo."

He took this with a good humored nod and gestured towards two dark oak chairs that waited on one side of the larger desk. He stood beside my chair, beaming that patronizing grin while I sat down slowly. The chair was clean, but I really wanted to pull out a tissue and wipe it down for no other reason than to pull some hot air out of that fat head. I heaved a mental sigh as I sat down. Years of training had ingrained a set of manners in me that wouldn't allow me to be that rude. At least not on a first meeting. The nuns would kill me. Beside me, Julie floated down into her chair, glowing.

A short silence settled on us as we stared expectantly at each other. I could see that whatever presentation Tino had planned, my not being a guy had definitely caught him off balance. Uncharacteristically for me, I decided not to wait for him to regroup but went on the attack.

"I understand you have approached my sister with a proposal for an investment." I had been on every side of these kinds of negotiations since I was seventeen, I knew the lingo. "Do you have a pro forma that I can take a look at?"

I buried a smug smile as I saw his patronizing grin freeze on his face.

"A what?" He wasn't nearly so self-assured right now.

"A pro forma. A detailed plan of what you want to do with the money, and how you intend to pay it back, and with what return on investment."

He glanced back and forth around the room as if to assure himself he was still sitting in his own office.

"This is a detective agency." He leaned forward as he whispered as if it was something I had overlooked.

I placed my elbows on the desk and my chin in

my hands, something I had never done in a business negotiation in my entire life.

"I figured that out," I whispered back. "All by myself. What I haven't got a clue about is why I should give you a red cent."

The grin disappeared and I wanted it back. There was a flash of anger in his eyes and I realized, a little late, that this could be a very dangerous man. A whole lot of my self-confidence decided to hide in my shoes.

His voice was ice cold. "I didn't *ask* you for *your* money. Julie *offered* to loan me some of *her* money."

I had a quick vision of concrete boots and a very cold Boston Harbor.

I shot a glance over to Julie, who smiled at me sheepishly. She hadn't bothered to tell me that. I took a deep breath. It was my turn to regroup.

"Okay, then. Are you offering any collateral?"

Tino slapped his forehead. Hard. I had never actually seen someone slap their own forehead. It looked painful.

"Um, Jo?" That note in Julie's voice told me that I might not like what she would say next. "There's something I think I need to tell you."

I looked from Julie to Tino and back to Julie, a sense of horror swallowing me up. "Oh dear God in Heaven," I whispered. "You're pregnant!"

"No!" Julie squeaked.

I stood up and looked at them again. Back and forth. Then light dawned. "Holy Mary, Mother of God! You're engaged?"

"No!" both Julie and Tino yelled so loud I jumped back. The look of horror in Tino's face was almost comical.

"Already married?"

"NO!" echoed the Geek Chorus.

I sat down again. "Okay, I'll shut up now. Just tell me what's going on before I have a complete nervous breakdown."

Julie glanced over to Tino as if to see if he wanted to start. He folded his arms and leaned back in his chair as if to say 'you're on your own here, kid'. Julie turned to me with her 'it's not as bad as it sounds' smile.

"Well, you know two months ago when I started those new voice lessons?"

I buried my face in my hands. For anyone else on the planet, voice lessons are voices lessons, but for Julie...

"Well, Mr. Sanderson told me I had real potential..."

...is there a bathroom nearby because I may vomit at any moment...

"...but he said that I needed performance experience in order to develop my stage presence..."

The buzzing in my head began to drown out Julie's words, but that was okay, because I could fill in the cracks.

"...so he arranged this gig for me in Japan..."

Okay. So it's true. My sister managed to find the only voice teacher in Boston who was moonlighting as a procurer for a Japanese white slavery ring. I don't know why I was surprised. It was practically inevitable.

The white dots in front of my eyes grew larger and Julie's voice faded. I felt a strong hand on my neck, forcing my head down between my knees.

"Take a deep breath, now hold it," a low voice was whispering in my ear, "now exhale."

The dots shrunk, I could see my legs again, and the world stopped spinning. I went to raise my head but the hand on my neck was insistent. "Not yet. Relax just one more minute."

The room had returned, but all I could see of it was the floor between my legs. I was suddenly very aware of the warm hand on my neck holding me immobile. The feeling of helplessness freaked me out. I twisted my head free and looked up to glare at him.

Okay, maybe it was a moment or two too soon. The room spun and I grabbed the edge of the desk. I took another deep breath and saw Tino, leaning back in his chair, looking like he was trying hard not to laugh at me.

Nothing like a small flash of temper tantrum to drive away any lingering vertigo.

"Then what happened?" I asked Julie after a flaming glare at Tino.

This time, it was Tino who deigned to answer. "I was working for a family from Swampscott to recover their daughter who also took lessons from the same voice teacher. It wasn't hard to see that whatever happened to Bella Abramson, the same thing was about to happen to Julie."

Julie bubbled as she interrupted Tino. "So when Tino walked up to me at the airport and asked me if I wanted to be a spy, I said 'Sure'! I mean, I can be a rock star anytime, but how often do you get a chance to be an international espionage agent!"

Tino grinned and shook his head. "Not an international espionage agent, an undercover operative."

"Whatever," Julie dismissed Tino's correction with a wave of her hand. "It was still very cool! I got to wear a wire and a GDS…"

"…a GPS…"

"And the U.S. Embassy in Tokyo was involved and the Tokyo police and there was a gun battle and people were killed and it would have been an international incident but they hushed it up and it was the most cool thing I've ever done!"

Julie was breathless with elation, while I was just breathless from hyperventilating. I thought about putting my head between my knees again, but a movement from Tino gave me a fresh flare of adrenaline and I forestalled his assistance with a sulking glare. He leaned back in his chair, folded his arms over his chest and made practically no attempt to hide the fact that he was laughing at me.

The urge to hit him was almost overpowering.

"So, having dragged my sister halfway across the globe, having put her in mortal danger, having encouraged her to behave in a way that anyone with two functioning brain cells would have known was wrong, you want me to repay you for almost getting her killed by giving you money?"

I had succeeded in wiping the grin off his face. If I hadn't been so angry, I probably would have been frightened by the cold rage in his eyes. Julie leapt into the breach.

"No Jo, you don't understand! Teeny says I'm real good at this, that I have a real aptitude."

At the urgent note in Julie's voice, I broke off from glaring at Tino. There was an earnest look to the set of her jaw that I had never seen before. For the first time, I saw a little of our father's strength in her.

"I know I'm not smart like you, Jo…"

I opened my mouth to contradict her, but she cut me off.

"I've never been good at stuff like school or business or anything important. But I can be good at this. Real good, right Teeny?"

Tino's grin was both warm and a little twisted as he gave a faint nod. "Actually, she was amazing. She's a consummate actress, she thinks on her feet very well and she never once panicked, even when the …um… situation hit the fan."

I could believe that. Julie had no sense of fear or mortality. Horrible things could happen all around her, but she just couldn't imagine that anything bad would ever happen to her. I compensated for her obliviousness by worrying about her twice as much as I worried about myself. She was giving me ulcers and now she wanted to go work as a detective.

Mental note: Buy stock in Maalox.

I looked closely at Julie. It never occurred to me that it might bother her that she was never any good at academics. If she was lame at math, then she made up for it at gym. And if she never made honors, she did have the most boyfriends. Since I had envied so much the things that she excelled in, and she always seemed so cheerful, I had no idea that she might feel inadequate. The voice lessons, the horse breeding scheme, that low budget movie that turned out to be a porn flick, these were all her efforts to feel accomplished. And I had never noticed.

I was a bad sister.

"Okay." I said, surrendering to my guilt. Again. "How much?"

The long smothering silence after that question did nothing to make me feel better. Julie looked at Tino, her tilted head echoing my question. Evidently, they had never discussed details. Tino wouldn't meet my eye. He almost squirmed in his seat. I bit back a smile as I got this quick vision of a ten year old Tino trying to lie to a nun. He had that same kind of look in his eye, like a guilty schoolboy.

"Five hundred and thirty six thousand," he said quietly after a small sigh.

Now it was my turn to be speechless. It didn't last however. It never does.

"DOLLARS?" I asked, not yelling. I don't care what anyone else may tell you, I did not yell. I simply asked.

Tino met my eye with a stony nod.

"No collateral, no pro forma, no business plan, and you want over a half a million dollars? For what?"

"Well, it's a little complicated."

I held up my hand to stop him. I did my eight second rosary followed by my three second yoga meditation. I took a deep breath. I could handle this. I lowered my hand. He continued.

"I'm in a bit of a bind. I had a business venture that... didn't go well." He stopped and looked at me, as if weighing how much to tell me. I think he decided to empty the whole grocery bag, because he stood up and grabbed a stack of large, battered envelopes from the top of one of the disreputable file cabinets. He lumbered back to the desk and sat down.

"About a year and a half back, one of my cousins decided that he wanted to enter the private investigation business. Expand it to include corporate security and internet fraud. You know, bring it in to the twenty-first century."

"That actually sounds like a good idea," I said. "What happened?"

"We leased some space in a fancy building in Government Center." Tino's voice was flat and dry. "Invested a load of money in expensive desks and state of the art computers, dropped a small fortune into advertising, and sat on our butts while the phones were as quiet as death and the entire venture went ass up in about six months."

His eyes were aimed on a spot on the wall but I could see they were focused on something that wasn't even in the room. There was a cold anger in his eyes that made me shiver, but there was also a flicker of despair as well.

I surprised myself by the mixed feelings that were being flamed by that little flicker.

With an apparent effort, Tino shook off his funk and focused back on us.

"We pulled the plug and defaulted on our lease and the loans, but I had signed a personal guarantee and now they're coming for the house."

"The house?"

"The house." He made a gesture that seemed to include not only the office we were in but the five floors above.

"You own this whole building?"

He nodded.

"Problem solved," I snorted with relief that I could be off the hook. "In the current market, this building is probably worth over two million. Sell it, pay off your debts and you'll still have over a million to start over with." I did a quick mental inventory of my purse, my jacket and my keys as I started to think about leaving.

"I can't sell the building." There was a note of finality in his voice that irritated my natural tenacity (not to be confused with pig-headedness, no matter what anyone else may tell you).

"What do you mean, you can't sell it. You're

going to lose it anyway."

"I can't lose it."

I whooshed out a long exasperated sigh. This was like talking to Julie. Rational words were not penetrating.

Without warning, Tino's hand whipped out and grabbed mine. His fingers wrapped around my wrist like a handcuff. There was no pressure, but his fingers were like a steel ring that I couldn't break free of. And if I gave a little shriek as he pulled me to my feet and dragged me to the door, I'm sure I could be forgiven.

"C'mon," he said as we walked out onto the street and then up the stairs into the first floor vestibule. He shot a look at Julie as she rose to follow. Julie must have understood whatever that glance meant, because she nodded and sat back down.

"I'll wait here," she said with a little smile as Tino dragged me out to the street.

CHAPTER FIVE

I paused as we walked into the wall of aromas that filled the foyer. Garlic and oregano and that smell of tomato sauce that suddenly reminded me of my Nana. I could hear muffled voices coming from behind doors, both near and far. As my eyes adjusted to the dim light, I saw a dusty beam of sunlight that plunged down from an old fashioned skylight at the top of an antique rectangular stairwell five stories above. Everything was in dark natural wood, dented and worn from decades of use. Scraps of clothes and a couple of towels were flung over the banisters. Faded old pictures decorated the walls. On the landings, battered upholstered chairs huddled under little floor lamps. Small bookcases rested against the walls and magazine racks nested next to the chairs.

"'Morning, Tino!" spoke a squeaky voice. I leapt in alarm since it appeared to have come from the upholstered chair in the foyer. As I looked closely, I saw a very old, very tiny woman, wearing a flowered housedress that blended almost perfectly with the back of the chair.

"GOOD MORNING, AUNTIE LOU!" Tino bellowed.

Auntie Lou pulled herself up out of her chair. She was so old and bent that her head stayed the same height from the floor as she hauled herself to her feet. She beamed at the two of us. "No need to yell. I can hear as well as I ever did. And who would you be?"

I extended my hand as Tino answered loudly. "THIS IS... MS. D'ANGELO."

I shot a glare at Tino before I turned to smile at Auntie Lou.

"You can call me Jo."

"You're a commie ho? Now is that nice language? You should be ashamed of yourself!" With that, she waddled into one of the doors that opened off the foyer and slammed it behind her with a resounding boom before I had a chance to respond.

My mouth opened and closed, but nothing came out. I turned to look at Tino, who was enjoying this much too much. Another door opened on the foyer and out stepped a tall plump dark woman with a huge brown beehive hairdo. She wore a pastel floral sweat suit with a worn and stained apron over it that read in huge letters: "Kiss the Cook!"

"Mama. This is Jo."

I glared again. I know I wasn't being consistent, but he really annoyed me. I turned to shake hands with her, but she surprised me by grabbing me in a smothering bone crushing hug.

"Good to meet you. Are you hungry? Look how

thin you are. Dinner is at one o'clock. You be sure to come. Tino, she's so skinny!" She shook her head, pinched my cheek and disappeared back into her apartment before I had a chance to speak.

"Uncle Luigi and Auntie Lou live in there," Tino's hand flicked towards the other door that Auntie Lou had disappeared into as we walked up the stairs. "You'll meet him at dinner."

I gave a start of surprise. I hadn't planned on staying for dinner. I opened my mouth to protest, but Tino kept right on with the tour. Like a piece of litter flying in the wake of a truck, I followed him up the stairs.

"My cousin Sandra and her three kids live there. Her husband does too, when they're talking to each other. Aunt Carla and Uncle Vinnie are across the hall."

A door opened on the landing above us to reveal a middle aged man with a sleeveless stained tee shirt that barely covered a hairy chest and a substantial pot belly. He leaned over the railing.

"So. Is this the Russian prostitute we've been hearing about?"

I turned on my heel and started back down the stairs, only to have my arm grabbed as I was spun back.

"My cousin Frankie, who lives here when he's not in jail."

Frankie found this very funny. His laugh sounded distinctly evil as it echoed up and down the stairwell. "Not fair!" He sputtered. "I haven't been convicted once!"

"Eighteen arrests, no convictions."

"You can call me 'Mr. Teflon'."

"Nice to meet you... Mr. Teflon."

Frankie laughed again, even louder, then belched before retiring back into his doorway. Across the hallway, another door opened. I was starting to feel like I was on that old T.V. show "Laugh-In" where everyone kept opening doors and throwing out one-liners.

The door opened a crack and I saw an eye peer out.

"Ha!" barked a voice in disgust and the door slammed shut with a snap.

"Auntie Maria. Technically she's a cousin, but everyone calls her Auntie."

A thud, thud, thud brought my eyes up to the third floor where a nearly naked toddler thumped on her diapered behind down the stairs.

"Jenna! Have you escaped?" Tino took the stairs two at a time and scooped the child up in his arms.

"Unka Ino! 'Scape!" the tiny voice echoed.

"Whoa!" Tino held the child at arm's length as the smell of ripe diapers overpowered the aroma of garlic and pasta sauce.

"Jenna!" a feminine voice bellowed from above. I glanced up and saw a harried woman about my age, in jeans and an oversized Boston Celtics sweatshirt, emerge from yet another door and glance frantically around.

"Down here," answered Tino.

She glanced over the railing, rolled her eyes and trotted down the stairs to meet Tino halfway. She scooped Jenna from his arms and placed her on her hip, seemingly more aware of her own messy hair than the diaper disaster in her arms.

"Hi," she said with a frank smile and an extended hand. "I'm Tino's sister Stephanie."

"Steph and her husband Bud live on the fourth floor with their two kids. Number three is on the way."

"Bud is an animal." Steph grinned and crossed her eyes. Her smile was infectious and I laughed as well. "Three kids in three years. He's killing me!"

Somehow, I didn't think so.

"I'm Jo." Okay, so I let Tino off the hook on that one. I wouldn't look at him, but I could feel him smirking.

"You coming to dinner?"

"I… um…"

"She'll be there. Her sister too," Tino said with misguided confidence.

"Oh good. I promise I won't be such a wreck and the kids will be clothed."

She disappeared back into her doorway, chatting to Jenna in baby talk.

Tino turned and headed back down the stairs. "My cousin Billy has the apartment across from Steph, but he's overseas with the Marines right now."

I shot a glance over my shoulder up to the top floor.

"I have the apartment on the fifth floor. I've got some storage up there as well."

The trip down the stairwell was relatively uneventful. Auntie Maria again peeked out of her apartment.

"Ha!" she barked again, but this time didn't close the door. Instead, I could feel her eye on my back until we descended below her line of vision.

As we headed out the front door, I heard Mrs. Scollari's voice echo through the stairwell. "One o'clock! Don't be late!"

I stood on the sidewalk and turned to look back at the building. I took a deep breath. I felt like I just escaped from a tempest, or maybe I was just in the eye of a hurricane that would suck me in again if I dared to go back in for the threatened dinner.

"Now you see why I can't lose this house." Tino said quietly.

As I stared at the building at 64 Salem Place, some of my father's words came back to me.

"Real Estate," he once told me, "is not about boundaries and deeds. Sometimes it's about soil and streets, but not often. And don't go thinking it's all about location, location, location. Real Estate is about people. It's where they live and work and play and love. Numbers are one thing, but don't go mixing numbers up with people."

This from a man who once made six million dollars in one day on one real estate transaction.

I remember listening to him and nodding sagely and not having a clue about what he was talking about. But that day, as I stood on that cracked sidewalk, I began to get an inkling.

I turned to look at Tino and found him staring at me with an intent look in his eye. I was puzzled. I couldn't read him. I couldn't like him. Yet I knew I was going to have to at least try to help.

I opened my mouth to answer when the sound of a gunshot froze the words in my throat. I could feel the blood drain out of my face. Julie! Left her alone! In Tino's office! With a coat rack dripping with guns! What was I thinking of?

CHAPTER SIX

Tino didn't bother with the five steps. He vaulted over the railing and yanked open the door to his office in one movement. Despite my modest one inch heels, I needed all five steps and raced in behind Tino, nearly plowing into his back.

Julie sat sheepishly in the chair where we had left her, her hands folded demurely in her lap. A Glock 9mm semi automatic rested on the desk in front of her and a slowly settling cloud of dust marked a new hole in the pitiful file cabinets.

"Sorry," Julie chewed on her lower lip. "I didn't think it was loaded."

Tino walked to the desk and picked up the gun. He checked the chamber and returned it to its holster on the coat rack. He sat down behind the desk and turned calmly to me. "You were saying…?"

Despite my decades of experience with Julie, it takes me more than a fraction of a second to recuperate. I twitched spasmodically for a moment before taking a deep breath. Eight second rosary. Three second yoga. Another deep breath. Okay. I can sit down now.

"Let me see those papers." I extended my hand

toward the stack of envelopes that sat on the desk.

Tino pulled them back from my fingers. "Say 'please'."

I glared and he wisely decided not to press his luck. I snatched them from his grasp with more attitude than grace.

The return address on the first envelope caught my eye. The real estate firm of Hogan O'Halloran. My face flushed hot and I heard my teeth grind together.

"You know O'Halloran?" Tino watched me intently.

I nodded faintly. "In the world of New England real estate, Hogan O'Halloran is known as the Dark Avenger. He takes it as a compliment, but it's not. The Dark Avenger is an internet worm virus that sneaks into your computer replicates itself until all of your files are gone. Hogan O'Halloran is a real estate worm virus. When O'Halloran gets his toe into a neighborhood, he replicates his soulless projects until he has wiped out every ounce of character and humanity. His grandfather worked on the old West End development." I looked Tino in the eye. "Hogan O'Halloran is one of the four sentient beings on this planet that think that Boston City Hall is attractive. And possible the only one who thinks that it could be improved with just a little more concrete."

Tino shuddered appropriately.

"But he is *so* hot!" Julie blurted out.

Tino and I stared at Julie for a moment and she

gave a little half shrug of apology. I turned my attention back to the papers in my hands.

"He is the antichrist of the real estate development world." I said. And I didn't have to mention my fears if he ever managed to infiltrate the North End. I opened the envelopes and began leafing through the pages. Scollari and Sons had taken out a five year lease on one of O'Halloran's properties on New Chardon Street. The lease documents were all standard, slightly exorbitant, but nothing that couldn't be supported by attorneys. I paged back through them again, puzzled.

"Where are your responses?"

"My what?"

"Your responses. The documents that your attorney filed to dispute these claims."

Again, we had the six foot four inch guilty schoolboy in front of me.

I sighed heavily. "You never filed any responses?"

"Why would I? I signed a personal guarantee and I couldn't make good. I just thought he'd give me more time, or that I could get a loan against this property. But he's screwed up my credit so badly that I can't get a bank to even talk to me."

If I sighed one more time I was going to hyperventilate. I rested my forehead into my hands to think. When Tino said he was desperate, he wasn't kidding. The documents in front of me showed that we had less than four days before

O'Halloran could force a foreclosure. By doing nothing, Tino allowed a process that should have taken years to speed through in six months. And it was so far along that it was entirely possible that even throwing money at it wouldn't fix it. O'Halloran wanted this building and I was just as determined that he wouldn't get it. The thought of little Jenna being homeless in her dirty diapers made me spitting mad.

I blew out a large gust of air (not sighing… just breathing) and cradled my head in my hands. Nothing was coming to me. I reviewed the documents again. Nothing.

"Jo will think of something." Julie whispered to Tino. "She always does."

Evidently misguided confidence was contagious.

I tossed my head back against the chair. My eyes weren't focusing as I stared out into space, but something niggled at my brain and my eyes wandered over to a framed certificate hanging on the wall.

"You were in the military?"

"Marines. Six years."

"Hoo-rah!"

"That's 'Hoo–ah!'"

"Whatever. Honorable discharge?"

"From active service. I'm still with the Reserve."

A beam of light! I straightened in my chair.

"When was the last time you did active duty?"

Tino shrugged. "I did my two weeks about a

month and a half ago. And about six months ago I ran a paramilitary training session in Indiana."

I quickly paged through the documents again, a sense of elation filling me.

"Is this good?" asked Julie.

"This is very good." I said with a smile. I reached for my phone and dialed my office.

"Attorney D'Angelo's office," I heard Rhonda, my legal assistant, answer.

"Rhonda, Rhonda, Rhonda!" I said in a merry sing-song voice.

"Well, you sound like you're about to swallow a canary. What are you up to?"

"Not a canary, Rhonda. But I am about to take a little bitty bite out of a vulture."

"Oh, fun! Can I play?"

"Sure! Could you pull up Suffolk docket MDB1133-82?" I read the info off the papers in my hands.

I could hear the tap tap of Rhonda's fingers as they danced on the keyboard of her terminal. "Oh, Hogan O'Halloran! Yippee!" she croaked happily.

Sometimes Rhonda and I have much too much fun.

"I need you to fill out a 10-26 SSA and have it filed at Suffolk district court within the hour."

"Soldier's and Sailor's Act? Is it applicable?"

"Possibly not at the other end of this litigation, but O'Halloran never served Scollari with the notice and he's a Reservist. It will set the entire litigation back to square one."

Rhonda chuckled gleefully. Everyone hates Hogan O'Halloran.

"When you get the court papers back, have a set of copies couriered over to O'Halloran's office with a letterhead identifying Chandler, Chandler and Bishop as the attorney of record representing Scollari. Oh, and Rhonda?"

"Yes?"

"Have the courier include a single red rose, with my compliments."

Rhonda and I were both giggling as we disconnected. And some people don't think that real estate law can be fun.

"Enjoying yourself?" Tino was watching me with a puzzled smile on his face.

"Today is turning out to be a very good day."

Tino waited patiently while I reveled in the deviousness of my machinations.

"The Soldiers and Sailors Civil Rights Act of 1942 prevents any bank from foreclosing or any landlord from evicting a tenant while they are in active duty."

"Yeah, but I'm just in the Reserve right now."

"Certain rights still apply and O'Halloran was obliged to notify you and publish that notice. He probably didn't do it because he didn't want to flag your attention to the fact that you have a legitimate defense against forcing the foreclosure of your principal residence. At the worst we've bought you a couple of years of litigation. At the best, we can try to get a judge to throw out the entire judgment.

That's the outside hope. I'm betting we can get the court to reduce the judgment and then we'll settle."

I smiled at Tino as I watched him visibly unwind. I had a quick image of Atlas, straightening his back, and watching the weight of the entire planet roll to the floor.

"Well, that deserves a celebration." He glanced at his watch. "And since dinner is almost ready, would you like to join us, *Ms.* D'Angelo?"

The cork popped off my bottle of euphoria. Real estate law I could handle. Taking on the Dark Avenger I could handle. Going back into the maelstrom of the Scollari "house" for dinner... I wasn't sure about that.

"Um, well, I need to get back to the office. There are things that I, uh, need..."

"Oh c'mon Jo!" Julie chimed in. "Mama Scollari make a wicked good spaghetti sauce, better even than Nana's!"

My back stiffened. Though the memory was old, I refused to admit that anyone could possibly make better pasta gravy than our Nana.

The words, "No, I really need to be going..." weren't out of my mouth when the bionic handcuff reached out and latched onto my wrist again.

"How can you defend your grandmother's sauce if you don't compare it?" Tino taunted as he pulled me out of my chair. He pulled me close and he bent his head to whisper in my ear. "Scared?"

I shot him one of my icy stares and squeezed my hand into a fist so he couldn't feel it shaking.

Okay. Yes. I was scared. And not just of the threatened dinner. The feel of Tino's hot breath in my ear was sending a whole lot of very strange feelings running through me and I will admit to you that fear and confusion were high on that list. I am not a brave person. I am what is known, if you'll pardon the language, as a major chickenshit. And dinner with the Scollaris and Tino whispering in my ear were events that were way the heck out of my comfort zone. I twisted my arm in an attempt to free my wrist, with no luck.

"Oh, c'mon, Jo," sang out Benedict Julie who grabbed my other hand tugging me to the door.

Which is how I got sucked into the maelstrom of Mama Scollari's Tuesday afternoon spaghetti dinner.

CHAPTER SEVEN

I sat stock still with my hands gripping each other on my lap, a smile tightly wired onto my cheeks and my brain registering some serious delays in processing all the data coming from eyes and ears.

The dining room of Mama Scollari's apartment was about as large as the dining room at my father's house in Cohasset. That, and the fact that there were tables and chairs, were the only points that these two rooms had in common.

Looking at the breaks in the wainscoting, I could see the faint clues where, years ago, someone had ripped out the walls separating the kitchen from the dining room and the dining room from the living room, making all three rooms into one large hall. The molding had been painted white and showed all the dings and scars that a well used room might expect to bear. The wallpaper above the woodwork was a faded yellow and white floral print, yet very little of this paper could be seen behind a vast collection of framed snapshots and family memorabilia that covered the walls. Greeting cards were wedged into picture frames and taped alongside photographs. Birthday cards, Mother's

Day cards, even Christmas cards, despite the fact that we were halfway into May, were everywhere. And some looked like they had been up there for decades.

Despite my frantic yet subtle maneuvering, I ended up sitting next to Tino. Julie sat on his other side and little Jenna was placed next to me, seated on top of dog-eared copies of the 1993 Boston Yellow Pages and the 1998 Boston White Pages. She squirmed as she turned to inspect me critically. I smiled uncertainly at her. My experience with children was practically non-existent. I have no close cousins with kids, and my get-togethers with my friends from school who are now mothers have always been their excuse for having their time away from their interesting offspring. So we can add talking with two year olds onto my "outside-the-comfort-zone" list.

"I sit grown-up table." Jenna declared soberly. At least that's what I think she said. A couple of consonants seemed to have dropped en route.

"I see," I replied. I felt that my response may have been a little insufficient, so I added, "How long have you been sitting at the grown up table?"

In hindsight, it was probably not a brilliant idea to ask a two-year-old complex questions that require conceptualizing time.

Nonetheless, after a moment of baffled silence, Jenna rose to the occasion with an animated monologue of which not one word could be understood as being in English.

I was way outside of my comfort zone.

Stephanie came to my rescue as she fastened a dishtowel around Jenna's neck with a clothespin. "Hush, Chattermouth!" she said, affectionately patting Jenna's lips with two of her fingers. Jenna obediently stopped talking and squirmed back to face her plate.

My relief was short lived as Stephanie dropped one dishtowel on my lap and laid another over the shoulder of the charcoal grey Prada suit I was wearing. I looked up at her, baffled, and she shot me a twisted smile as she said, "Trust me, you'll need them."

Oh, boy.

The dining room table was actually four different tables of various widths and heights that had been placed side by side and covered with one ten yard length of yellow checkered fabric. Sixteen chairs were lined around the table, another half a dozen were standing sentry in various locations around the room and a stack of folding chairs leaned against an antique china cabinet, apparently waiting for those occasions when there were would be more than twenty two people for dinner. Not counting the folding chairs I counted nine different styles of chairs.

"And what would your name be, dearie?" asked Auntie Lou, apparently having completely forgotten our earlier introduction. Her head barely reached over the top of the table. Someone should have given her a couple of phonebooks to sit on as well.

"I thought this was your Russian prostitute, Auntie." bellowed Frankie with a wink in my direction.

"Hit him." Auntie Lou muttered and Mama Scollari obediently reached out and smacked Frankie across the back of his head.

"Watch your mouth!" Auntie Lou's finger trembled as it wagged at his impudence. "There are children present. Besides, the whore had red hair, this one has brown."

I gazed longingly at the door to the hallway as Mama Scollari placed an enormous platter of spaghetti and meatballs on the table. Julie, apparently at home in this chaos, lifted the bowl, pulled a couple of heaping forkfuls onto her plate, and passed the platter to Tino, who filled his plate until you could barely see the rim of his dish. I grabbed a small serving of pasta and quickly passed the platter over Jenna's head to Stephanie who stopped to plop another pile onto my plate before splatting a small mound onto Jenna's dish.

"Don't worry," said Steph with a smile. "Mama's got plenty more on the stove."

Truth be told, I wasn't being thoughtful. I just didn't think I could get any more than a couple of mouthfuls down.

Stephanie reached over to cut up Jenna's spaghetti and without thinking, I inched my plate away from her just in case she got the idea that I needed my food cut up as well. I had the feeling that Steph thought of me as another one of her children. I began to worry that at any moment someone was going to give *me* a phonebook to sit on.

A short hush fell over the table as everyone dug in. Evidently, the first few mouthfuls of food are more important than conversation. I took the moment to check out those faces around the table that I hadn't seen before.

Mama Scollari sat at the head of the table, closest to the stove, and spent most of the dinner getting up and down refilling the pasta, the cheese, the meatballs, the sausage, the milk, the Chianti, the water pitcher, the butter, the napkins... it went on and on. By the end of the meal there was as much food on the table as when we started.

At the other end of the table, Sandra presided like an amateur lion tamer surrounded by her three half-wild children who spent much more of their energy trying to kill each other than actually eating any food.

Seated beside Stephanie, enthroned in a 1960s vintage battered high chair, young Sean reigned, gibbering merrily and banging utensils as Stephanie shoveled dabs of baby food into his busy mouth. He looked a bit like a changeling with his bright copper curls and sea-green eyes. Everyone else in this family looked so Italian.

Stephanie switched gears frequently, chatting gibberish to Sean, baby talk to Jenna, and small talk to me.

42

I was very impressed.

"Da goo boy!" she cooed, shoveling green and orange slime into her child's mouth. "Use your spoon, Jenna. So, Jo, what do you do? Jenna! Spoon!"

"I, um, work as a real estate attorney at the firm of Chandler, Chandler and Bishop."

"Wow, that's cool! Open up wide! Do you work in Government Center?"

"Yes, that's where our main offices are, but we have satellite offices in the suburbs as well."

"One more!" (I think that was to Sean) "Is Tino working with you on a case?"

With a spastic wave of a loaded spoon, Jenna sent a wad of minced spaghetti flying through the air to strike my cheek before landing neatly with a splat on the strategically placed dishtowel.

"Uh, well, I'm working on some real estate litigation for him." I answered, wiping my face with a napkin.

"Oh, good! Jenna! Eat, don't play! He needs someone to look after the business end of the business. He's great with drug dealers and homicidal maniacs, but he just cannot balance a check book."

I glanced over at Tino, who methodically shoveled spaghetti into his mouth, seemingly uninterested in our conversation but I suspected that he heard every word. I looked over to Julie, but she was talking with Mrs. Scollari.

Now I know that some people go for decades

without balancing their checkbooks, but in my mind, that's in the same category as being homeless. Something has to be seriously wrong. I had this chilling flash of being sucked into something that was way over my head.

I gulped half a glass of Chianti before remembering that I don't drink red wine. I gave a convulsive gag and a glop hit my skirt. I blotted most of it up, trying not to think how much André, my dry cleaner, was going to howl about the stain.

An hour later I stood twitching on the sidewalk, smiling goodbye to nearly the entire Scollari family as they arranged themselves on the steps to wave me off. It reminded me of the Beverly Hillbillies, times four, with Auntie Lou perpetually hunched over like Granny to wave between the closing credits.

That had to have been the most frightening meal of my entire life.

CHAPTER EIGHT

With cool composure I smoothly engineered my escape, my car ka-thunking over the curb, off the sidewalk and down Salem Place, leaving only one orphaned hubcap rolling down a desolate back alley.

There was no way I was going back for it. It was on its own.

Pulling into the parking garage, I felt the rollercoaster in my stomach start to slow down. The chaos of the Scollari Family and the wilderness of the North End began to fade into a manageable memory, an obscure deviation from the calm, controlled civilized tranquility which was normally my life.

By the time I walked into the office, it was nearly two thirty. I was lucky that I was way ahead on my billable hours quota for the month. I wouldn't want to have to explain to Frank Bishop what I had been up to all morning.

This might be a little hard to avoid if he happened to drop by my office since I had a little surprise waiting for me when I got there.

"Got a delivery today," Rhonda announced her voice suspiciously impassive. I raised my eyebrows at her but she met my look with an innocent gaze that looked completely unnatural on her face.

Of course, there was very little that was natural about Rhonda Broomfield. From her banana yellow hair that screamed lime green under the fluorescent lights, to the Cleopatra eyeliner that ran right out to her hairline and probably wrapped around her the back of her head, I doubted that there was anywhere on this planet where she would blend in. She tended to coordinate her colored contact lenses to her two inch long fingernails, which might not have been so unnerving if currently her finger nails weren't detailed with tiger stripes. This week, her contacts were tiger eyes which made her look like an alien from some late night cable sci-fi show. Combine that with the tiger-stripe skin-tight almost-a-dress that she had worn yesterday, and it's not surprising that the courier had fled from the office, crossing himself and muttering in Spanish as he raced for the stairwell, choosing not to wait for the elevator but running down eleven flights to the safety of the street.

I get the same urge sometimes when I see Rhonda. Unfortunately, I don't speak Spanish.

If my assistant belonged on "Freaks Up the Night", then my office was evidently the movie set for some film noir horror flick. I walked in to find that someone had delivered some forty or fifty bouquets of roses. As an added touch, they had cut off all the blossoms and spray painted the stems black. It felt like I was walking into a burnt out forest.

I stood in the doorway in shock. A very bad feeling, like an ice cold spider creeping up my back, made me twitch.

"Very… Tarentino," I said at last, trying to be cool. My mouth was as dry as I wanted my voice to sound. But it didn't. It sounded a bit shaky. I gave myself a mental dope slap and pulled myself together. I didn't want Rhonda to see how badly this unnerved me.

"It's making me hot," Rhonda said, stepping beside me. I really wished she was being sarcastic but unfortunately hate mail in the form of dead foliage probably *was* a turn on for her. Lord knows, everything else was. She handed me a tiny white envelope.

I'm such a wimp. My hand shook a little as I opened it. I'm not good at confrontation and I think I just invited a covert corporate terrorist action into my office.

"Fuck off, Bitch."

It was so neatly lettered too, in bright red ink with that overly studied penmanship that made me think that whoever had written it might have gone to the same Catholic school as I had. For a moment, I focused on the fluidity of the handwriting and in my mind I could hear Sister Benignus' voice droning, "Down and curve and cross and there's your 'F'. Now smoothly up and down and there's your 'u'…" I shook my head violently. Sister Benignus would kill me if she knew what my mind was making her spell.

"Forty two of them."

Rhonda's voice brought me back to the office. I looked at her curiously.

"Forty-two identical decapitated bouquets with forty-two identical notes."

"Nice. Elegant without being tasteful. Hogan O'Halloran?"

"You tick off any other vindictive maniacs this week?"

"I don't think so, but it's only Tuesday." I walked to my desk. Rhonda started to clear the botanical carnage.

"Don't bother," I said. "Just call Maintenance and have someone come up and clear out the cadavers."

I heard the door click behind Rhonda. I picked up a file, sat down and stared at it without seeing. My right leg started to twitch in a delayed shock. I pressed my hands down on my knees and took a deep breath.

I'll admit it. I was shaken. I thought about the amount of rage needed to go out and execute a gesture this dramatically malicious. I don't think I'd ever had that much anger directed at me, personally, before. And, yes, it was just a little freaking me out.

Eight second rosary. Three second Yoga. Deep breath. Okay, then.

I reached for the file on the Jerginski closing and tried to bury myself into the quiet refuge of an uncontested real estate transaction, but my mind wouldn't focus and my eyes kept straying to the blackened stems.

A token knock followed by the immediate opening of the door broke into my futile efforts to review the documents in front of me. I pushed aside the file in disgust. The Jerginskis were going to have to wait.

We were being invaded by the Ho Jo, the slut clone from the ninth floor.

For almost a year now, Lucy Rudd had been administrative assistant to my fiancé, Phillip Gorson. I had tried hinting to Phillip that Lucy might be a little too presumptuous, that her overly familiar manner was not the least bit endearing to me, but was in fact, more than a little rude. Phillip had just laughed and tweaked my nose.

"Honey! She has a crush on you! She idolizes you! She imitates everything you do! I think it's cute."

I rubbed my nose in disgust. I hated it when Phillip tweaked my nose.

"It's not cute!" I had told him. "It's a little bit freaky and I wish she'd stop."

Lucy's so-called crush on me had manifested itself in a very disconcerting way. Within a month of being hired on as Phillip's assistant, she had gone to the beauty salon and had her hair cut, colored and permed to match mine, though hers looked a lot redder than my muted auburn. She went on a diet and worked out at the gym and lost ten pounds. Since she was about an inch taller and one full cup size bigger, she ended up with a much better figure than me.

And she spent far too much of her salary buying wardrobe to match mine. If I found a nice little Brooks Brothers suit on sale, she'd go out on her lunch hour and buy one just like it. Once, just to see what she'd do, I wore a plaid lime green and pink jacket and skirt set that I had picked up at a church bazaar but insisted that I had bought at Macy's. For three consecutive afternoons she disappeared at lunch, coming back around three o'clock reeking with failure, depression and desperation. I probably would have broken down and confessed, but on Monday morning, didn't she saunter in wearing a lime green and pink plaid skirt suit.

And, damn, didn't it look good on her. I figure she must have bought the material and pattern and sewed all weekend.

One of the biggest thrills of her life was to be mistaken for me from behind. Pitiful.

And by the time she had leased a silver Lexus GS identical to mine, the whole "crush" thing had gone beyond cute, past annoying and well into to the realm of weirdness. Lucy Rudd completely freaked me out.

I don't know who had first nicknamed her "Ho Jo", Rhonda swears it was me, but I would never say anything that rude. Out loud. But wherever it had come from, it had stuck and behind her back she was known throughout both law firms as "the

Ho Jo".

She now stood in my doorway like some vapid clone. She was wearing a Bergamo suit that was almost the same color and cut as the charcoal gray Prada suit that I was wearing. I winced. I hate it when she guesses right and we look like twins.

"Phillip says for me to ask you…" She broke off as she stared in amazement at the budless bouquets that decorated my office.

I winced again. Lucy's voice was high-pitched and whiney with a Somerville-Medford accent. She didn't snap gum when she spoke, but the effect was the same.

"He wants to know if you's want to go to Amici's for dinner tonight."

Damn. I liked Amici's. It would be quiet and dark and relaxing with really good food, but it was also in the North End and I couldn't take two North End Italian dinners in one day. I shook my head emphatically.

"Tell him no thanks. Another night maybe. I was out of the office most of the day and I'll be working late to catch up."

I bent my head back to my papers, hoping she would take the hint and leave.

Who was I kidding? She walked in and started fingering the foliage.

"Oops. Sorry," she giggled as a blackened leaf snapped off and fell to the carpet. "What's all this about, anyway?"

I kept my head down and bit my lip. "Oh this?

It's the latest trend in office decoration. I saw it in Architectural Digest last week." I looked up and gave her my best just-between-us-girls look. "It's supposed to be symbolically erotic!"

"Really?" She looked around at the number of vases that lined the cabinets and windowsills. "Jees!"

"Very trendy."

"Cool."

I smothered a grin as I thought about what Phillip would say when he came into his office tomorrow to find dozens of blackened flower stems garnishing his file cabinets. It would be good for a laugh.

A long silence did not lead me to believe that Lucy had left. I sighed and lifted my head. Lucy was edging her way to my desk.

"What?" I asked.

"Um, nothing." She leaned over and wrinkled her nose. "I was just wondering what perfume you wear."

"Safari, by Ralph Lauren." I lied quickly but immediately regretted it. What if Phillip had sent her down here to figure out what scent I wore so that he could get me a present? "But Fendi is nice too."

There. I now had a fifty-fifty chance of either getting a good present or having the Ho Jo start to smell like me.

"Right." She turned for the door.

"Um, Lucy?"

She stopped and looked back.

"It's 'Lucienne'." She pronounced it with a French accent as she tossed her hair off her shoulders.

"Whatever. Next time, let Phillip call me himself."

"Oh, he was gonna," she beamed cheerfully, "But since I was heading down here, I figured I'd just ask ya for him!"

I floundered for a moment, unable to come up with a response for that.

"What an exceptional assistant you are," was all I could come up with.

"Thank you. I try." She left smiling, completely oblivious to sarcasm.

Rhonda was nowhere to be seen in the outer office, which explained how Lucy got by. I left my door open so that I would hear her when she got back.

I was deep into the Jerginski closing when I felt rather than heard someone else's presence. I looked up and saw a large figure filling my doorway.

Hogan O'Halloran was an attractive man, in a studied and contrived sort of way. His expensive tweed jacket opened up to reveal a beige mock turtle neck jersey stretched tight over the impressive abs which showed just how much time he spent at the gym with his personal trainer. When he had first heard about his nickname, the Dark Avenger, he had dyed his hair, which I suspect was originally a light reddish brown leaning towards gray. He now had thick brown-black curls. He dyed his brows to match, but his lashes, which framed pale blue-grey eyes, were a strange reddish-blonde. It gave his face this very weird I'm-not-from-this-planet look.

It seemed that nearly every year Boston Magazine named him as one of the top ten bachelors in New England. Too bad they didn't know a little more about him. Keeping three different girlfriends in three different states should really disqualify any guy from being considered an eligible bachelor, regardless of how much money he's got.

He leaned on the doorframe, crossed his arms over his chest and stared at me. A cold smile creased only one cheek; the other side of his face didn't seem to want to be bothered.

I sat frozen, looking up to the door, pen in one hand, papers in another, surrounded by black stagnant stems. My mind was a complete blank. I couldn't think of a thing to say. No polite greeting, no clever quip, no glib barbed insult. I just sat there staring at him.

Six hours later (okay, maybe thirty seconds) and the silence had still not been broken. I could see O'Halloran was trying for a power play, but for me, what started as being speechless with stupidity had evolved into pure obstinacy. I was not going to be the one to break this face off.

But I *was* wondering what had happened to Rhonda.

Finally, I leaned back in my chair and slowly

laid down my pen. I picked up the small model phone booth that I kept on my desk and turned it over in my hands.

Maybe O'Halloran took this as my having blinked first and stepped into the room. Whatever. The cold war was getting old anyway.

"Did you like my flowers?" His voice was smooth with an icy smirk.

"Oh, are they from you?" I was going for the wide-eyed innocent version of sarcasm. "I thought Tim Burton had branched out into interior decorating."

The smiling half of O'Halloran's face decided to make a little more effort.

I could feel my right cheek smirking back. I remember how Julie would make different faces in the mirror to see how she looked when she was trying to be cool. I always thought that was slightly insane of her, but now I wished I had practiced leering. I had the unsettling feeling that I looked like a doofus.

O'Halloran cut to the chase. He pressed both hands on my desk and leaned his face until we were nearly nose to nose.

"I don't remember inviting you to play in my sandbox." His voice was soft and almost sweet, in a singsong sort of way.

"Just as well," I whispered back, "'cause I've been told that playing well with others has never been one of my life skills."

The smirk left his face and he stared at me. He

was so close that the scent of his breath was stronger than his cologne.

"Corned beef and cabbage for lunch?" I asked politely.

His nose twitched and his eyes narrowed. I watched him without moving until his arm lashed out. His fist punched the vase that was about twelve inches to the left of my face. I jerked back as the vase flew off the desk, spilling water and scraps of foliage everywhere.

Okay. Are we happy now? We now have an open display of physical violence. Are we satisfied?

My hands moved slowly onto my lap so that they would be hidden by the desk as I clenched my knees. I could feel my heart beating like a rapper's bass, but I was fighting to keep my breath even and to keep meeting his eyes. Having provoked him this far, I thought that maybe keeping my mouth shut right now might be my best move.

There was enough venom in his voice to down an elephant.

"Don't fuck with me, D'Angelo."

God help me, I couldn't resist.

"The thought never entered *my* head." I did the tiniest glance down to his crotch. "Has it entered *yours*?"

When am I going to learn to keep my mouth shut?

A noise from the outer office brought O'Halloran's nose back from to a safe distance from my face. The cavalry had arrived.

"Darryl from Maintenance can't make it up here until after five pm so I grabbed Carlos from..." Rhonda's voice broke off when she saw my visitor. Her mouth gaped melodramatically and she froze in the doorway.

"We'll finish this discussion later." There was a note in his voice made me think that the next time the discussion might not be quite so cordial.

"Call first. I might have something more important to do."

O'Halloran scowled and would have stormed out of the door, but Rhonda was still there, blocking his dramatic exit. He could have squeezed by except that Rhonda, never one to let an opportunity slide by unredeemed, did one of those grabby-gropey excuse-me pardon-me bits in which she managed to both snag a handful of butt as well as rub her boobs all over him on his way out.

She stood in the doorway, torn between stalking her prey down the hall and interrogating me as to what she had missed.

Curiosity won out over lust this time, probably because the odds were fairly certain that she wasn't going to get another stab at his buns if she followed him, but it was a near sure thing that she could bludgeon some juicy gossip out of me.

I straightened the papers on my desk and ignored the deafening silence for as long as I could. I held out for almost five seconds.

"Nothing very interesting." I answered her wordless question, not making eye contact. "He just wanted to be sure I knew that the flowers had come from him."

"And????"

"We talked about what he had for lunch, and then you came back, and he left."

Rhonda glared at me. She was good at that. She'd have made a good nun. Except for her clothes. And her makeup. And her hair. And her language. Oh, yeah, and she'd have to give up the whole sexual predator thing. So maybe it's just as well she didn't go the nun-route.

Rhonda turned to go back to her desk, muttering as she left. "Damn, and I could have cornered O'Halloran in the elevator."

She slammed the door so loudly that the vases on my desk shook. As the bouquets' tremblings settled, mine kicked in.

My legs went seismic. I sat with my hands clutched in my lap, forcing down the bile that was threatening to toss spaghetti and meatballs all over the Jerginski closing. Maybe I just wasn't cut out for corporate power games.

Since I was seventeen, my dad had let me sit and watch whenever he had any of his "more interesting" meetings. Joseph D'Angelo loved the battle. Sometimes he'd open with a frontal assault. Sometimes he'd start out gentle and passive, luring his opponent into a false sense of superiority. But I could read Dad like a book. I knew just when he was about to pounce and I would get such a thrill of pride when he'd go in for the kill. Well, maybe it was a little bloodlust, but I tell you, it wasn't hard to imagine how Dad could have been a blood-thirsty warrior in another age.

A couple of years ago for Father's Day I bought Dad a small cast-bronze model phone booth for his desk.

"What's this for?" he'd asked.

"It's for when you make the change from a mild mannered businessman into a Roman gladiator."

I smiled at the memory of how big his laugh had been. And ever since that day, he'd kept the little phone booth on his desk, picking it up as a seemingly idle gesture just before he turned the tables.

When he died, I'd thought about putting the little phone booth into his casket, but later I was glad that I didn't. A lot of things kept my memories of my father alive, and that miniature bronze phone booth was one of them.

As I turned the little statue over in my hands, I wondered once again about why he had me sit and watch.

The obvious reason sprung to mind. Not having a son, he'd wanted me to learn the business, and more important, all the tactics and strategies that he'd developed over the decades of playing the game.

I used to wonder if my sitting there quietly, not speaking, barely moving, was also one of Dad's little tactics. Not very fair I suppose, but it may have stifled some of the more aggressive maneuvers that his opponents might have used if I had not been there. Particularly if they had daughters of their own at home.

But I think the real reason that Dad wanted me there was because he loved the audience. As rewarding as the fight itself might be, the amazement and the applause of an appreciative spectator was his biggest incentive. And I was definitely Dad's number one fan.

But I wasn't my father. My father never sat with his shaking fingers clenched into fists, fighting nausea after a business meeting. After the battle, my father was high on adrenalin, almost giddy, and had to restrain himself from dancing on his desk.

I wanted to hide under the desk and suck my thumb.

CHAPTER NINE

I talked with Julie on the cell phone on the ride home from work. By the time I finished telling her about O'Halloran and Rhonda and the budless flowers, she was laughing so hard that I began to smile about the whole thing myself.

"I have GOT to tell Tino about this! He will laugh out loud!"

Hmm. Sounded like she was getting serious about Tino. I had mixed feelings about that and I wondered if it might be time for a big sister chat.

"Do you want to come over for dinner tonight? You know Ant Bee will have made enough for a family of six."

"No, I told Tino I'd have dinner at his place. I'm on my way now. Do you want to come?"

Definitely sounding serious but nothing short of a .38 revolver pointing at my head was going to drag me back into that mayhem.

"Um, no thanks, I'll probably pop over to Phillip's later." Okay, a little lie, but my day had already been as frenetic as I thought I could deal with in a twenty-four period.

We talked until I pulled up into the driveway, then I disconnected, grabbed the files that I wanted to work on that night, and headed into the house.

"Hi, Ant Bee! I'm home."

I feel a little stupid calling her Ant Bee, but it's what we've always called her.

Bertuska Czigany had been our housekeeper since I was thirteen and Julie was twelve. We'd gone through six housekeepers in five years and we'd pretty much accepted the fact that housekeepers lasted only slightly longer than chocolate ice cream in the freezer.

It was Julie that had dubbed her "Ant Bee", and I'll admit that she did look very much like a manic Hungarian version of Opie's aunt. She was about four feet six inches tall and almost the same wide with her hair pulled back into a bouffant bun. No one cared what she wore, but everyday she had on the same uniform: a grey maid's dress with a little white lace handkerchief in her pocket and a white apron around her waist. I think she took Alice on the Brady Bunch as her role model. I also think that she watched her on a black and white television.

Years ago, Ant Bee had defected from Hungary, smuggling herself inside of a packing crate, nearly suffocating and almost freezing to death in a valiant effort to get to America and freedom. Three weeks later the Berlin Wall came down and the Soviet Union collapsed making her entire ordeal somewhat pointless.

To this day, she spits on the ground every time someone mentions Ronald Reagan's name.

She bustled into the foyer, smelling like freshly

baked bread and muttering in Hungarian as she took my briefcase. This is what she used to do to my father when he came home and after he died, she started doing it to me. It's a little annoying but I figure she's probably just worried about finding a new job at her age.

I looked down at the top of her head as she tried to wrestle my suit jacket off me. I never let her take my jacket, but she still tried every night. When she had first arrived fourteen years ago, her hair had been a rich dark brown with only a few scatterings of grey. Now it was nearly pure white. Dad had left her ten grand in his will, but that's really not enough to retire with and so she stayed on.

My footsteps echoed as I walked into the dining room. I sat down, noticing for perhaps the first time how really big this room was. I had seen it set for thirty people, but that was when Dad was alive. But even when it was just Julie, Dad and me, it had never seemed overly large. It was just the way it always was. Tonight though, it felt hollow.

And quiet. Nice and quiet.

I reached for my briefcase and pulled out the file that I was working on.

"You have no bring friends to dinner?" asked Ant Bee as she wheeled in enough food to feed an Olympic Sumo wrestling team.

She asked the same question almost every night. You would think that at some point she might get the grammar right.

"No, Ant Bee," I answered as I reached for the

Kressler closing file. "Just me tonight."

"A friend you need is a friend you feed." She said as she tottered back to the kitchen.

Ant Bee was fond of quotes, though she rarely got them right.

I poked at the veal cutlets as I stared at yet another cookie cutter purchase and sale agreement, racking my brains to find some adjustment to justify the fees we were charging. The sound of the surf distracted me and I put down the fork and the file and leaned back in my chair, listening to the waves slapping the seawall.

My father had bought this house when I was seventeen. I smile about it now, but I remember how melodramatic I was back then. My summer boyfriend had dumped me and I refused to go back to the Cape that June. How could I ever step foot in Hyannis again now that Alex and I had broken up? I laughed out loud. I hadn't even thought about Alex for years, but he had been my first crush, my summer love for two summers in a row before he sent me a typewritten "Dear Joan" letter. I had been devastated. I had moped around for weeks, swearing off all men forever.

I guess the brochure that I got in the mail from the Archdiocese, "So, you want to be a nun?" kind of panicked my father. Dad had sold the house on the Cape and quickly bought this house on the beach in Cohasset. We moved out of the townhouse in Back Bay and into this beachfront colonial about thirty miles south of Boston.

It had worked too. That was the summer I started dating Phillip.

I met Phillip at one of those teen mixers at the Cohasset Country Club that parents think are safe because someone's uncle is pretending to be a chaperon when he's actually over in the bar hitting on one of the waitresses. Unfortunately, loud music, dim lights and groping hands just can't overcome the impression that you were trying to party in what felt like your grandmother's living room.

I was seventeen, sitting with Julie stirring a glass of diet coke that they dressed up with small bits of produce to make it look like it's got alcohol in it.

There had been a time when Julie was going through her awkward ugly adolescent stage when her hair was horrible, she was gangly and goofy looking, and had really bad acne. Unfortunately for the rest of the female half of the human race, that phase had only lasted about two months. By sixteen, Julie was tall, slim and had that long straight blonde hair that make people turn and stare.

I had long since resigned myself to another evening of being mistaken for part of the upholstery when a tall lanky figure seemingly dropped out of the ceiling tiles, having leapt over the back of the bench seat to land with a wuff of complaining vinyl between the two of us.

"I must be dead and this must be heaven, because where else can you find angels as beautiful as you two."

Okay, Phillip later admitted that he got that from a book of pickup lines, and despite the fact that he actually acknowledged my existence, my first impression was that here was a man interning to be an asshole.

"And what did you die of? An allergic reaction to polyester or an overdose of Binaca breath spray?"

Gee, and I wonder why I have trouble getting dates.

By some freak of contortion, Phillip had managed to get his arms over both our shoulders while still managing to turn his back on me. My dulcet little banter however, did manage to get him to glance back at me.

"Gee, isn't your little sister cute."

Julie bit her lower lip and glanced down at her drink. She knew exactly how much it irked me to be mistaken for the younger sister. I'm sure they'll be in a time when I get really old, like my mid-forties, when I might revel in something like that, but at that moment, I was just pissed.

"Yes, well, thank God we live in America where everyone has a right to be a moron. However, I'm a little concerned that you might be abusing the privilege."

The arm came off my shoulder and I got the full exposure of the back of his head.

"Okay, then again, maybe not. I think I'm changing my mind," he said to Julie.

"Hey, when you go to get your mind changed,

you should think about swapping out the rest of the head at the same time. You couldn't do worse." I glanced around, looking for an escape route.

This surprised a laugh out of him and he actually turned to face me. Carl DiRocci, who had been circling our table like a Sunday driver in a packed parking lot, took this opportunity to dive in and pull Julie out on to the dance floor. And yes, I was kind of tickled that Phillip hadn't seemed even remotely bothered. It was almost as if he wasn't disappointed to be stuck with me.

So we dated our final year of high school and went to each other's proms. He went to UMass Boston and I went to Boston College. We both studied pre-law and we both went to Suffolk Law School. He got his J.D. in criminal law while I studied the safe and boring real estate law. After graduation, getting engaged was so implied that it was pretty much anti-climatic. He gave me the ring on my birthday and his mother was so happy, she had palpitations.

Phillip's mother loved me. Truth be told, there were some days that I liked Phyllis more than I liked Phillip. She took me shopping and brought me to her hairdresser and laughed at everything I said.

And Dad and Mr. Gorson had been friends. On Tuesdays afternoons they would play golf together and on Friday nights they would play poker. They did some joint real estate developments together and belonged to the same clubs.

Yes, the pending Phillip and Josephine merger

had the unanimous approval of all interested parties.

We were supposed to have been married a year ago September, but we postponed the wedding after my father died in a car accident and for some reason we both just got too busy with our careers to re-set the date.

By the time I finished my carrots I was regretting blowing off Phillip. Take-out Chinese food and a couple of hours on the sofa watching a rented movie would have been definitely more interesting than veal cutlets and the Kressler closing. With a slap of my hand I closed the file and got up from the table.

I grabbed the "Pride and Prejudice" DVDs despite knowing perfectly well that the only way Phillip would suffer through them was if he were bound, gagged and semiconscious, and started to the door.

Ant Bee wandered in with an apple turnover with a six inch peak of whipped cream. Frankly, I think Ant Bee always went heavy on the whipped cream so she could huff the canister when it was empty. She shook her head with disapproval as I grabbed my car keys.

"In! Out! In! Out! Where you go now?"

"Oh, um, I think I just might, um ..." Why does she make feel like a teenager sneaking out on a school night? I'm an adult. A professional business woman. A lawyer. If I want to go over to my fiance's for a little sofa snuggle, that's my business. I took a deep breath and said in my most assertive tone of voice, "I'm going over Phillip's for the evening. If, um, that's okay?"

Okay, maybe not as assertive as I could hope, but it's a start.

Ant Bee grumped over to the dining room table and began to clear away the dinner dishes. "Umph. Well, remember what they say. 'Why buy the stone when you can get the moss for free.'"

"Okay, Ant Bee. I'll remember." I had no idea what she was talking about. "Don't wait up. Goodnight."

I made my escape. I cranked up the radio and pulled out of the garage, and in minutes I was headed back up Route 3A towards Boston.

CHAPTER TEN

Phillip lived in a waterfront condo in a renovated wood frame multi-family on Savin Hill in Dorchester. Everyone had rolled their eyes and shook their heads when he bought it because Dorchester had a well-deserved reputation for being more than just a little bit dangerous. Phillip didn't care. He had gone to college around the corner at UMass and his old frat house was nearby. And living on the edge of a dwindling ghetto was as close to living on the edge as Phillip Gorson was ever likely to get.

From the balcony of his third floor condo, you could see the Atlantic Ocean in one direction and the Boston skyline in the other. The neighborhood looked beautiful; if you didn't know better you'd think you were in Back Bay or Beacon Hill. I parked a block away, next to Savin Hill Park, touched up my lipstick, grabbed my little tube of mace out the glove compartment, and headed up street.

I hadn't called first. I wanted to surprise him. As I used the keys he had given me to get in the front door and walked up the stairs, I played out a half a dozen cute and endearing opening comments to dazzle him with. Highly rehearsed spontaneity.

That's my specialty.

I had barely opened his door when I stopped dead in my tracks. From somewhere inside, I heard gasping and grunting noises, as if someone was having an epileptic fit. I rushed in, passing by the standard issue chaos that always decorated Phillip's condo. Chinese food boxes on the coffee table, scraps of clothing on the couches, bottles and glasses on the TV and the bookshelves, I tore past them in a panic, hurrying to the bedroom where I could hear the sounds of someone gasping in pain.

I must admit that for a full second, my first thought was, my God, Phillip has a hairy butt. Then my next thought was, my God, Phillip has four legs.

I stood staring at this tableau without moving for hours. Well, minutes. Okay, probably seconds, but it seemed like hours. For some reason, my mind had a major problem processing what my eyes were seeing.

Even when, with a grunt and a wheeze, Phillip's hairy butt shifted to the side and I caught the glimpse of a pair of large breasts that had been pinned beneath his chest, I still could not fully comprehend the scene in front of me.

My god, I can't believe how hairy Phillip's butt is.

Now it may seem that I was obsessing a bit on this, but you've got to understand, I had yet to see Phillip's naked butt. And Phillip is fairly hairless. He has a little chest hair, but not much. And his arm and leg hair is as fair as the hair on his head, but my

God, he had such a hairy butt. It looked like he was wearing a brown monkey fur speedo. I stood there staring with the same frozen morbid horror that you would have when you come up unexpectedly on a bad car wreck on the expressway. Arms and limps everywhere, but your mind just can't process the carnage.

I glanced over to the dresser where I saw one of those hinged three-photo frames displayed on the top. The photo in the middle was the one with Phillip and me at the Topsfield fair last fall. The one to the left was one of me in my bathing suit on the sailboat and the one to the right was my graduation portrait (the one without me squinting). They were all aimed so that they had an unobstructed view of the gymnastic events that were happening on the bed.

I suddenly had this completely irrational burst of maternal instinct towards those pictures. They really shouldn't be watching this. As I walked over to the bureau, I couldn't help but wonder what other events they might have witnessed from this scenic vista.

It was then that I noticed that there were black, budless flower stems strewn all over the bedroom. They had even made a very nice wreath of them around my pictures.

What a pair of sickos. I glanced back to the bed. It didn't take a magna cum laude to figure out who the visiting team was, even if both sides were dressed in "skins".

I thought it a bit weird that my hands weren't shaking as I lifted the pictures from the bureau. I don't know if it was the clatter of the frames or that I had just moved into his line of sight, but with a gasp, Phillip rolled off the mattress, arms flailing, trying to block my view of the bed.

"AAAAAAAAAH!" he screamed, (E-flat over middle C).

"EEEEEEEEEHHHH!" I screamed back, (G-sharp over high C, modulating down to E-flat).

By the time we were done screaming we were almost in perfect harmony, possibly for the first and last time in our relationship.

From the bedsheets came an obnoxiously nasal familiar whine.

"Shit, Jo! I thought you said you were working late tonight."

Lucienne Rudd, aka the Ho Jo, pushed herself to a near sitting position, leaning back on her elbows so her substantial C-cup breasts were pointing directly at me. The tone of her voice was neither guilty nor repentant. It was more as if she was annoyed at me for showing up and was looking for me to apologize for barging in.

"Wow," I said conversationally. "You have really ugly nipples."

Actually she didn't, but that comment at least managed to not only shut her up but to encourage her to cover said nipples (and the rest of her torso) under the sheets.

"Ab... duh duh... ma... eeeh... umm... ba

73

uh…" Phillip sputtered.

You know, if Phillip could be that articulate in the courtroom, he could probably afford a condo in a nicer area.

I was amazed at how calm I was acting. Maybe I was in shock. Whatever the reason, I found myself staring at Phillip's crotch.

"It's not polite to point," I said calmly and then turned and left the room.

I have absolutely no memory of leaving the condo, walking down the stairs and out to my car. My next memory was sitting at a red light on Morrissey Boulevard. The light had changed but I didn't move.

All of a sudden I started to shake. I shifted the car into park. I wasn't crying. I was shaking and my nose was running and my vision was blurry with tears, but I wasn't really crying. Just shaking. And leaking.

Cars were beeping, drivers were passing me, offering single digit hand gestures of encouragement out their windows. But I didn't move. I couldn't. I couldn't even see, never mind drive.

My cell phone rang. I looked at it. Phillip. I disconnected him. Two seconds later, it rang again. This time I powered it all the way off and tossed it in the back seat. Then I let out a scream so long and so loud that my throat hurt. The guy in the next car rolled down his window to yell at me, but then took one look and wisely decided against it and drove on.

By the time the light changed red again, I started to get a grip. I rooted around in the glove compartment for the tissues, blew my nose, dried my face (separate tissues), and shifted my car into gear.

Unfortunately, the light hadn't changed to green again, a fact which several ever-so-helpful car horns quickly reminded me. I slammed on my brakes, inches from a collision, my heart pummeling painfully in my chest.

I drove home slowly, driving like an old lady, so drained that I almost felt like I was drunk.

I parked in the driveway. I didn't want Ant Bee to hear the garage door opening. I wasn't in the mood for any more moss analogies.

Two hours later and I was still sitting in the dark on the back deck, wrapped up like a troll in a quilt, listening to the ocean and trying to figure out what the hell I was feeling.

The quart of chocolate fudge brownie ice cream that I had stopped to buy at the Cumberland Farms store was half eaten. The last half was a brown miasma that was dripping slowly out of the bottom of the carton, making a sticky mess on the wood deck.

My eyes weren't focusing as I made swirls in the chocolate soup with my spoon. I had gone well past shock before even clearing Quincy. I had run the gambit of murderous rage, shame, embarrassment and emotional desolation. I had even dabbled briefly in guilt, but I wasn't in the mood to be stupid. Despite the best efforts of the nuns to instill me with an overactive sense of *mea culpa*, there wasn't a chance I was taking the rap for this one.

Unless it <u>was</u> my fault? Maybe I hadn't been affectionate enough? Maybe we shouldn't have postponed the wedding? Maybe we should have set a new date? Maybe I shouldn't have been such a prude? Maybe I should have put out?

Screw that.

It was close on to midnight when a realization hit me like a boom to the back of the head.

I felt relief. Under all the crap, I felt like I had just been released from a cage.

How horrible am I?

On the water, the reflection of a quarter moon pointed an accusing finger at me. You are a horrible person, it said. You led Phillip on. You never wanted to marry him. You are a horrible person.

So it <u>was</u> all my fault. Go figure.

Even my anger for the despicable Ho Jo was fading. There was a tiny germ of emotion buried deep. I dug it out and looked at it.

Gratitude. Omigod, a very small part of me was actually grateful to that obnoxious slut. A very, very, very small part. A part so small it was much too easy to bury it under the layers of anger and disgust that I still felt for the two of them. Yet nonetheless, I had this urge to compile a Phillip Gorson Maintenance Handbook and mail it to the

Ho Jo, along with the keys to his apartment with a note that said "Take him. He's all yours."

I picked up the ice cream carton, tossed it into the trash, stuck out my tongue at the moon and then went to bed.

I'm a repressed Catholic. I can't sleep with my fiancé, but I can sleep with guilt.

CHAPTER ELEVEN

In the morning, I found my breakfast already set out on the table and a scrawled note from Ant Bee propped up next to the plate of toast.

"Gone shooping. The early bird gets the porn."

I swear to God, that's what it said.

Note to self: check cable bill. What premium channels are we paying for?

An hour later, I was pulling into the garage at work.

"Hi Barry", I waved and smiled at the security guard. Barry was about a hundred and seventy years old. If anything criminal ever happened in the parking structure, we'd all be dead. It took him two or three minutes to get his walkie-talkie out its holster. And let's not even talk about working the buttons. I wonder why they won't let him carry a gun.

Barry sat, as was his habit, on a beat up nylon lawn chair with a forty ounce cup of coffee and a nine-month old copy of the National Enquirer. He looked up when I called, but instead of his normal "Hey, cutie!" he just stared at me blankly.

I smiled at him anyway. I guess you have to conserve what brain cells you've got left when you get to be that age.

As I walked into the lobby, Carlos, the concierge and Marcia, the security Amazon were in the middle of a quiet, intense gossip. They broke off when they saw me. Their eyes widened and they glanced back at each other, as if amazed to see me.

I nodded a greeting as I walked by, but I started to feel a little uneasy.

Then the elevator doors opened and Jimmy Diodati, one of the attorneys from Phillip's office started to step out, but then he caught sight of me and froze.

"Eeep!" he squeaked.

"Hi Jimmy?"

Jimmy did one of those squirm moves to avoid me like I had joined Scientology and he didn't want take the flyer.

Now I was completely freaked out. I pushed the button for the eleventh floor as light dawned on Marblehead.

They all knew! Oh. My. God. Everyone in the building, from the cleaning staff to the partners of the firm, they all knew about last night!

I was pretty certain that Phillip wouldn't spread it around. After all, it could totally screw his chances to become a partner.

SHE had to have told everyone. Ho Jo, that diseased cow whore. First she spreads her legs with my fiancé, and then she spreads the news all over the building. I could kill her with my bare hands.

I hit the button for floor nine. If the elevator

hadn't stopped, I might have tried to rip open the doors with my nails.

I can't remember ever being that mad before. I could barely see. I blasted out of the elevator like a bomb had detonated behind me.

My entrance was as dramatic as any Hollywood diva could ever plan, but I couldn't care less. There were more people than normal hanging about the office but, as if on cue, all their chatter stopped as soon as the saw me. My feet pounded on the carpet as I passed cluster after cluster of gaping morons, heading for Phillip's office and the Ho Jo's desk.

The rancid cow wasn't at her desk and it was apparent that she hadn't been in that morning. Probably exhausted from putting in all that overtime last night, poor thing.

I stopped dead for a moment. If it wasn't the bovine bitch that broadcast it all over the building, then it must have been Phillip.

If I had been angry before, I just blasted into supernova. Anything remotely resembling common courtesy disappeared as I crashed into his office, slamming the door closed behind me.

Under his sprayed-on suntan, Phillip's face paled about eight shades until his skin blended in with the off-white walls behind him. My vision wavered in fury. All I could see was a gaping mouth, glazed eyes and the strip of dark blond hair across the top.

A beige man, sitting across from his desk, rose at my entrance and wisely backed away. I barely noticed him.

"You told!" I screamed.

"You thought I wouldn't?"

I couldn't believe it. Phillip's attitude was the picture of outraged virtue, as if *he* were the injured party.

"Are you out of your mind? Why would you spread it around? Even if we completely overlook any consideration you might ever have had for *me*, this could cost you your chance at a partnership!"

"And saying nothing could get me disbarred!"

The blatant stupidity of that comment left me speechless. I had this flash of a vision of what the Massachusetts court system would be like if they disbarred every lawyer who lied about infidelity.

Actually, the world might be a better place.

"I can't believe your audacity!" Phillip ran his fingers through his hair. "To walk in here, acting like it's all my fault!"

My mouth hung open so long my tongue started to dry out.

"Are you actually trying to blame ME for what happened last night?" My voice squeaked with rage and shock. "Even for a self-centered prick like you, that's a stretch!"

Phillip had the look of a cornered rat who was trying to rant his way free.

"Well, better a self-centered prick than a frigid cock-tease."

"Monkey butt!"

"Spoiled brat!"

The air in my lungs turned to stone. I picked up the pencil holder off his desk and flung it at his head. He ducked and pens flew everywhere as it hit the window, bouncing all over the room.

"You take that back!" I could barely get my voice to work. "You take that back!"

"Ms. D'Angelo?"

I had completely forgotten about the beige man who had stood standing against the wall during this entire "discussion". I backed away from Phillip, my face burning with embarrassment.

The man was so non-descript that he was almost interesting looking. He was the kind of guy that you might meet a dozen times, but would be hard put to actually describe. That being said, he was medium height, maybe five-ten, with hair that was salt and pepper brown. His face was ordinary, his posture, unassuming. He wore tailored beige slacks, a muted dress shirt and a crisp tan trench coat. He looked like the kind of person that might result if Martha Stewart and Columbo ever had children.

Oh, brilliant. Now I have this mental image of Martha Stewart and Peter Falk doing the dirty. Strange, they're in Phillip's bedroom and Columbo has a hairy butt.

I slapped my face in a futile effort to purge the vision, but it was useless. It was burned into my psyche and would no doubt haunt me forever.

The beige man raised an eyebrow at me, but I wisely decided not to explain myself.

"Detective Ken McAdams," he introduced himself. "Boston Homicide."

Okay, now I feel even stupider, if possible. He was probably consulting Phillip on one of his cases. I made some inarticulate apology noises and, with one last death glare at Phillip, I started for the door.

"I'm working on an investigation and I'd like to ask you some questions." He pulled out a mini tape recorder and placed it on the desk.

"No, No. I'm just a real estate attorney," though I will admit that I was slightly flattered that he wanted my opinion.

"I'd like to talk to you about last night."

Warning: Temper shifting back into overdrive. I whipped around to face Phillip.

"Why don't you just take out a full page ad in the Globe?"

"I didn't need to." The sarcasm in Phillip's voice could cut diamonds. "They covered it for free."

"Don't you wish! You're not *that* interesting!"

"...er, Ms. D'Angelo?" Detective McBeige seemed a little unsure about whether he should interrupt.

"WHAT?" Okay, maybe not as polite as I could have been.

"We were just discussing how you shot Lucienne Rudd last night."

There was a calculating look in his eye that I might have been leery of, if I hadn't been too busy switching gears from raging fury to floundering confusion. Ho Jo? Shot? Me? Huh?

"I… shot… Lucy… Rudd… last… night?" I echoed his words in disbelief, trying to figure out what he was saying and if I had heard him correctly.

I wish I could say that I regretted saying those words as soon they got out of my mouth, but the truth was, I was so befuddled about everything that I wasn't even aware of how it sounded. Besides, I'm a real estate attorney. My knowledge of the criminal justice system comes more from watching "Law and Order" than anything I actually learned in school.

I was so busy trying to make sense of that bombshell that I wasn't even aware that he was still speaking to me until he grasped my wrist.

"Huh?" I asked, pulling myself back from the Land of the Clueless.

Detective McAdams sighed and started again. "You have the right to remain silent…"

"You guys actually say that? Like on T.V.?"

Again he sighed and restarted. "You have the right to remain silent…"

"If she does, it'll be a first." Phillip was standing, looking out the window, his back turned to me. His voice was monotone, seemingly emotionless. I glared at his back.

"Mr. Gorson, please." Yet beneath Detective McAdams polite impatience, I could sense a certain edge of excitement. Like a man who has just won the lottery and wants to keep it a secret.

Or a detective who has just tricked a murderer into confessing.

I don't actually remember hearing my Miranda Rights. And I don't actually remember him cuffing my wrists behind me. All I remember is Phillip's back as he stood staring out the window. He wouldn't even turn to look at me.

A tug at my arm made me realize that Detective McBeige was trying to lead me out, but I pulled back.

"Phillip?" My voice cracked and I forced a gulp of saliva down my dry throat. It didn't help much. My words came out like a whisper. "Do you know a good lawyer?"

He didn't speak. He didn't turn around. He didn't move. Maybe his shoulders shook a little. I couldn't tell if he was laughing or crying.

And I really didn't care.

CHAPTER TWELVE

"There are no seatbelts back here."

No response from the front seat.

"Isn't against the law not to have seatbelts?"

Still nothing.

"You know, if we stop short, my face is going right into that grill. With my hands like this, there's not a thing I can do to save myself."

Detective McBeige shot a glance over to the uniformed police officer behind the wheel. I got the feeling that they were toying with the idea of playing a little stop and go, just to shut me up. I decided to (finally) exercise my right to remain silent. I stared out the window, working hard to get a grasp on what was happening.

I hadn't thought that anything could be more humiliating than what had happened last night, but being led through Phillip's office and out through the lobby, my hands cuffed behind my back had completely eclipsed that. I hunched down in the seat, hoping that no one else I might know would see me.

The police station on New Chardon Street is, at best, a five minute walk from my office building, but due to the layout of the streets of Boston, it's a fifteen minute drive. First you circle City Hall, go through Haymarket, skirt the North End, only to drive past the foot of New Chardon Street since it is now a one way street coming towards you. You then go past Mass General, bang a left at top of the old West End and end up 200 yards from where you started, just so you can take a left turn on to New Chardon.

I used this time wisely, dividing my energies between feeling very sorry for myself and devising diabolical schemes of revenge against Phillip. It wasn't until Detective McBeige walked around the car to chivalrously open my door, that it hit me. (A revelation... not the door).

Sometime in the next hour or two, I would be given the opportunity to make a phone call and I didn't know who I was going to call.

Once upon a time, I would have called my father, but he'd been dead almost two years now. Yesterday at this time, it would have been Phillip, but that option expired last night.

God is inconsistent. Sister Benignus says that God works in mysterious ways, but screw that, God is fickle. Since He was obviously out to make me have the most horrible week of my life, He should just go the whole ten yards and make it a wet miserable day so that my hair frizzes and my mascara runs. As it was, by the time I got out of the police car, the photographer for the Herald got a wonderful picture of me in my salmon-colored Alfani suit. And I will admit that, at that moment, the thought in my head was, thank God it's not raining else my hair would be frizzing.

The inanity of my vanity kept my mind pretty well occupied right through the booking process, so I was no way near being ready when Detective McBeige pushed a telephone console at me that had more buttons than NASA.

"One call." He leaned back in his chair, not trying nearly hard enough to hide his smirk.

I stared at the phone. I wanted it to be one of the 1940's black phones with the dial. I wanted to be Hildy Johnson in "His Girl Friday". She always looked good, she always knew what to say and she was never frightened so badly that she wet her pants. I wanted to be Hildy Johnson.

Almost all my friends are lawyers, but I couldn't think of one that I could call. I needed a criminal lawyer, and every one of those that I knew either worked at Phillip's office or were friends of Phillip's.

Julie was a good one to call. If you have a craving for a hot fudge sundae, that is. Or needed someone to go shopping with. Or if you wanted to drive up to L.L. Bean in Freeport, Maine at two in the morning. I just couldn't think of what she would do if I were to call her about this.

McBeige's smirk was growing into a leer. I could feel myself sweating. I've never been one for acting on an impulse, but I was starting to panic.

"Can I borrow your yellow pages?" Damn. My voice cracked. Hildy Johnson, where are you?

McBeige's leer blossomed into a sneer as he dropped the tome in front of me with a loud thwack that made me twitch. I could see his curiosity rousing when I bypassed "A" for "Attorneys" and "L" for Legal Services and went straight to "P" for Private Investigators. His sneer faded quickly as my finger traced over the surprising short list of firms that were listed there. And his spine straightened and his eyes grew sharp when my finger stopped on the single line, bold face entry of "Scollari and Sons, Private Investigators". I don't know why, but I felt like it was my turn to smirk, so I did. I picked up the handset, punched an outside line, and dialed.

"Scollari and Sons, Private Investigators" answered a very feminine, very sexy and very familiar voice.

"Julie, it's Jo. Can I talk to Tino for a second?"

"OMIGOD!" I pulled the handset away from my ear to protect what was left of my hearing. "JO! I'VE BEEN TRYING TO CALL YOU ALL MORNING! WHERE ARE YOU?"

"It's a long story. I don't know how much time I have, so can I talk to Tino for a sec?"

"Why didn't you answer your cell phone?"

I instinctively looked down for my purse, but they had impounded it when I was booked.

"Oh," I said, remembering. "I turned it off last night and threw it in the backseat."

"Right." Trust Julie to understand totally irrational behavior. "Where are y... oh, here's Tino."

Tino's voice was clipped and abrupt, but

somehow I felt better hearing it.

"Where are you?"

"Police Station." Unconsciously, the pitch of my voice dropped to match his and I felt my panic level drop as well.

"Which one?"

"Government Center."

"I'll be there in ten minutes. Don't say a word to anyone. Wait for your attorney."

"Tino..." Panic level rising again. "I don't have an attorney for this kind of stuff." Actually I did yesterday, but let's not go there.

"I'll take care of that, just don't speak to anyone until your attorney arrives." He disconnected abruptly. What he lacked in phone etiquette, he made up for in confidence restoration. I sighed as I set the phone back down on the hook.

McBeige eyed me warily.

"You know Scollari?"

I picked up a pen off the desk and scrawled a note up the margin of the phonebook:

I've been advised not to speak until my attorney arrives.

I smiled sweetly as I watched Detective McBeige turn into Detective McBurn and hoped that, just this once, I could keep my mouth shut when I was supposed to.

৵৲৶

CHAPTER THIRTEEN

You wouldn't think that the booking bench in a busy police station could be such a lonely place.

I sat and watched as everyone went about their business. The room hummed loudly as dozens of officers, detectives, lawyers and even some real criminal-looking people came and went. No one even looked at me. Had they forgotten about me? I examined the cuffs that now bound my wrists in front of me. I wondered if I could pick the lock. I bet Hildy Johnson could have, but she probably had a hairpin. Did anyone use hairpins anymore?

The buzz dropped for a moment, then resumed at a slightly higher pitch. I looked around for the reason, but before I could figure out what had changed, McBeige appeared out of nowhere, grabbed my arm and led me down an echoing corridor into a small, stark room. He let me in but didn't enter himself. Then, without a word, the door closed behind me and I was alone.

It was a very small room, about eight feet by eight feet, but it wasn't a cell. Much smaller than the interrogation rooms on Law and Order, it had a small table and three chairs. I looked around for the two-way mirror and was a bit disappointed when I didn't see one, but there were little cameras in each corner, pointing into the room, so I wiggled my fingers at one and sat down.

I sat patiently for several seconds before taking another tour of the room. It was grey and boring and there were no magazines, and yet it was still nicer than the waiting room at my OB/GYN. Go figure.

Despite the luxurious amenities, I decided to try the door and was surprised when the knob turned. I opened the door a crack and peeked down the hall.

"I've got M.O.C., Scollari. Motive, Opportunity and a Confession." I could hear McBeige's voice echoing in the hall, but I couldn't see him yet. He sounded like he was trying to gloat, but there was an edge of uncertainty to his voice.

"Yeah, right." There was a hint of contempt in Tino's voice. "And we both know how well your 'confessions' stand up in court. How about a witness or a weapon?"

"We've got people combing the beach outside the Cohasset house and we're getting a warrant to search inside. She's got permits for sixteen guns, three of them are thirty eights, and that's what the murder weapon was."

I quietly shut the door as I saw the two of them coming around the corner and ran back to stand behind the furthest chair (which was about eighteen inches farther from the door than the nearest chair... like I said, small room.) The door opened quickly and Tino stood on the threshold, completely blocking McBeige's entrance.

He stared at me with a look of such cold rage that I instinctively pressed back against the wall. When he spoke, his voice was so menacing that I thought they ought to make him register his mouth as a deadly weapon.

"Get the cuffs off her. Now."

It took a moment to realize that his anger wasn't directed at me. McBeige, entering the room behind Tino, stopped to glare up at him, but must have decided that arguing might not be a good health choice. As he walked slowly over to where I stood and unlocked the cuffs, his eyes never came off Tino. They reminded me of two dogs fighting over a bone and I have to tell you, the bone does not feel very special under those circumstances.

Tino's eyes narrowed as I rubbed my wrists. Actually, the cuffs weren't on all that tight, it was more of an instinctive move.

"I want to speak to her alone. Her attorney will be here soon, but until then, I'm acting as an affiliate of counsel." Tino glanced up at one of the cameras and raised an eyebrow, meaningfully.

McBeige snorted and headed for the door, but whipped around in horrified dismay at Tino's next comment.

"When Mallory arrives, send her in."

"Sonofabitch… you called in *Mallory*?" McBeige sounded horrified.

Tino smiled unpleasantly as McBeige shook his head, sighed and then left, closing the door behind him.

Tino turned back to face me, his expression was unreadable. My back was still glued to the wall, no more certain than the rest of me as to what was going on inside his head.

"Don't worry," his face was like stone, his voice, like ice. "It'll be alright."

"ALRIGHT? I catch my monkey butt fiancé bumping uglies with the exclusive distributor of gonorrhea for the Northeast, who is then murdered and everyone thinks I did it, and then I'm arrested in the middle of Phillip's office and dragged out in cuffs with everyone staring at me and my picture's going to be in the Herald and at least it was a good hair day but I don't want to go to jail cause they make you wear orange jumpsuits and there isn't one shade of orange that's in my color palette. And you just stand there and say it'll be alright?"

At least that's what I was going to say. I'm not sure how much actually got out of my mouth in English because I had only managed to stutter out about ten syllables when I started to fall apart.

I had pretty much held it together last night and I had been fighting down the hysteria all morning, holding on to my self-control so tightly that my fingernails had made indents in my palms.

And now? Standing in front of the most annoying human being on the entire planet, now I fall apart?

Incoherent words jostled between hiccupping breaths. Two hands on my shoulders pressed my face into a sweater covered chest. I stiffened for a moment as a pair of rock hard arms wrap around my back. Then the nor'easter of trauma and drama that I'd been tacking through the last fourteen hours finally hit me and I collapsed sobbing like a three year old.

Tino's sweater carried the lingering scents of sea air, fabric softener, garlic and gunpowder. We were definitely in trouble because I happen to like all those smells.

I froze as two thoughts hit me at the exact same moment. (I can multitask like that... it's one of my few talents.) I was definitely getting much too cozy with my sister's new boyfriend. And my nose was leaking all over his sweater.

I pulled away awkwardly and looked around for a box of tissue. Not surprisingly, City of Boston Police interrogation rooms are not as well stocked with all the amenities as one might hope. I was seriously considering using the sleeve of my jacket when a handkerchief appeared in front of my face.

"Thanks," I mumbled gracelessly.

As I went to grab it, Tino knocked my hand away with his wrist and proceeded to wipe my cheeks.

"Blow," he commanded, holding the handkerchief over my nose. I was so staggered by his actions that I actually blew my nose. In the same handkerchief that he had just wiped my cheeks with. He then put the handkerchief back into his pocket and sat down.

"So," he said crossing his arms, "tell me what happened."

"I just blew my nose on the same handkerchief that you wiped my cheeks with."

His lips twisted as if he had something caught between his teeth.

"Okay. Maybe we can start a little before that…"

Oh. That.

I took a deep breath and sat down. I looked down at my hands and gathered my thoughts.

"Well, you see, Phillip and I have been dating since my senior year in high school--"

"Let's jump ahead to last night."

I don't care what he smells like. He is without doubt the most irritating man on the Eastern seaboard.

"I was getting to that. I just thought you might need a little background."

Whatever Tino's response might have been, we will never know. At that moment, the door slammed open and an earth-toned cyclone in the shape of a woman blasted into the room with all the politesse of a Patriot's fullback.

"Put away the rubber hoses! No more questions! The counsel for the defense has arrived!"

A large black woman, posed like an avenging angel, stood dramatically in the doorway. Her orange and brown African batik print sari matched the towering turban that she wore on her head and the huge gold hoops she wore in her ears matched the bangles around her wrists and the gilt choker about her neck. She was a tall woman to begin with, but with the ten inch high turban she was even taller than Tino. And while I wouldn't call her fat (to her face), she was definitely statuesque. This space- challenged room was getting a little crowded.

She looked around intently, as if searching for her prey. She huffed a disappointed sigh as she realized that it was only Tino and I in the room. She contracted from her diva pose and shrunk down to mere mortal size.

"And you must be... Mallory?" I asked, bravely breeching the deafening silence.

"Laticia Mallory Krutachia Benzani Jones," she announced, handing me her business card. "But 'Mallory' works too. Are you the innocent victim of the abusive and fascist corruption that they dare to call the justice system?"

"Uuuuuuum. I guess so." I hadn't really thought about it that way, but it seemed to fit.

With a regal flourish, Mallory enthroned herself in the last open chair. We now had me and these two goliaths crammed into three little chairs around a small table. I closed my eyes and took a couple of deep breaths to relax. When I opened them again, I found the two of them staring at me, looking puzzled and concerned.

"Just a little claustrophobia, with a side order of stress. I'll be fine."

"Right." With no D.A. or police officers to

intimidate, Mallory dropped the three quarters of her attitude and her manner became very matter of fact, almost soothing. "So tell me what happened."

"Well, last night after dinner, I decided to go over to Phillip's condo."

"Phillip?"

"Phillip Gorson. He's my... He *was* my fiancé." I clenched my jaw to keep from grinding my teeth.

"How long have you known him?"

I shot one of my piercing glares at Tino. I did <u>not</u> stick my tongue out, though the urge was strong.

"I've been dating Phillip since my senior year in high school. It's been..." I paused to do the math. "God, it's been almost ten years."

"What time did you leave your house?"

Again, I have to stop and think. "Maybe between six thirty and seven. Right after dinner."

Question. Response. Question. Response. I felt myself calming down as she methodically dissected the last fourteen hours, and also the last ten years of my life.

"When you got back home, did anyone see you arrive?"

"Well, no. I parked my car in the driveway so Ant Bee wouldn't hear the garage door. I didn't feel up to dealing with her."

"Your aunt lives with you?"

"No, she's not my aunt. She's the housekeeper. We just call her Ant Bee."

Oh jeez. There it was. The "La-ti-da... she's got

a housekeeper" look.

"Oh, don't look at me like that! She was my father's housekeeper and she came with the house. She's been there for almost fifteen years and I'm not going to be the one to put her out on the street just because I don't need a housekeeper anymore." Besides, I like not having to vacuum.

Mallory gave me the "don't get your panties in a twist" look and leaned back in her chair.

"And what time was that?"

How weird is it that you never really notice what time it is when you life is falling apart?

"I don't know, maybe nine or ten. I didn't look at the clock."

"Then what?"

"I sat out on the back deck feeling sorry for myself, ate a quart of chocolate ice cream, then went to bed. It was well after eleven when I went upstairs."

There was a silence as both Tino and Mallory exchanged looks. I don't think I was giving them enough to go on.

"I think it must have been pretty close to nine when I went out on the deck. The moon was only about ten degrees above the horizon when I went out there, and it was at about forty five degrees when I went inside."

Tino and Mallory turned to stare at me with various levels of disbelief.

"I sail." I explained.

This didn't seem to clarify things enough for

them.

"Boats."

Nope. Still nothing.

"You measure things like time and location from the stars and the moon when you sail at night. It becomes a habit."

I had this flash of memory of a teenage me, lying on the deck of my little skiff, cuddling with my then-boyfriend, Alex, as he pointed out the stars and the planets and explained how they changed with the seasons.

It must be the stress. I'd barely had a thought of Alex for years and now I'd recalled him twice in two days. I shook my head to clear it.

"Okay, then," Mallory looked down at the typewritten report that she had brought in with her. "So, this morning, when you said to Phillip, 'You told', you were referring to..."

"...the fact that he'd slept with the Ho Jo, and then announced it all over the building."

"The 'Ho Jo'?"

I had the grace to blush. "Sorry. 'Lucienne'. Her nickname was the 'Ho Jo'."

Tino had been silently listening to the questioning, but at this, he straightened in his chair.

"Why?" he asked, his eyes narrowing.

"Cause she had this really annoying habit of copying everything I did. She copied my clothes, she copied my car..." ...she screwed my fiancé... "she even had her hair cut and colored to match mine. It was the running joke of both offices."

Boy, didn't I sound petty and obnoxious. The woman was dead, for God sakes. Could I at least fake some sympathy?

Mallory paged through the transcript in front of her, a gleefully evil smile blossoming on her face.

"It fits," she chortled. "Each of your responses could fit those of a woman concerned about everyone finding out that her fiancé was cheating on her."

"That's because," I said slowly, "that's exactly what I was thinking."

"Even better!" she said. "So when you confessed to killing Ms. Rudd…"

"I didn't!" My voice cracked again. "I just didn't understand what he said. I didn't even know the Ho Jo was dead. I thought that she was just taking the morning off."

Mallory's smile was euphoric. "Perfect. We're ready to speak to the D.A." Her voice switched back to her ebonic accent. "You just stick to that story, little girl!"

She stood up and put her hand to the doorknob, pausing to remark over her shoulder, "Except for that Ho Jo crap. Drop that. Irrelevant and won't sound good to the jury. She was 'Ms. Rudd' or 'Lucienne'. Got it?"

She didn't wait for my answer, but drawing herself up to her full diva stature, she exited the room.

Despite the additional oxygen provided by her exit, I felt it difficult to breath.

"Jury?" I whispered.

I searched Tino's face for some reassurance that this was all a bad dream that would be ending soon, but his eyes were focused on the wall behind me. I turned, but couldn't figure out what he was looking at.

"Um... Tino? Hello?"

"Just thinking..." he said slowly.

I waited patiently but apparently nothing else was coming.

"Where's Julie?" I asked after three or four ~~hours~~ minutes of silence.

"I sent her out to do some leg work."

"Brilliant," I muttered, "I'm in jail for murder and she's at the gym working on her glutes."

That got his attention. He turned and laughed out loud, a huge, deep-chested bark that was almost frightening in its volume. He reached over and tousled my hair.

I pulled back. I wasn't sure if I liked having my head patted like a puppy.

"Good," he smiled. "Keep your sense of humor."

I wasn't trying to be funny.

He went back to doing his deer in the headlights imitation. He hadn't nearly enough time to perfect it before the door slammed open and Mallory returned leading the lynch mob. Okay, maybe it was only McBeige and another man, but I was pretty sure that with five people, we were exceeding the architect's original specs for room capacity.

Mallory moved around the table to stand protectively next to me. While this significantly reduced my already diminished personal space, it did leave me with a clear view of the new man as he entered the room.

He was tall and thin. His dark brown hair was professionally styled and a little grey at the temples added to his distinguished veneer. His suit was tailored to fit and he had that bronzed skin and gleaming white smile of a news anchor or a politician. He looked vaguely familiar.

"Scollari." He acknowledged Tino with a nod and a pepsodent smile that stayed on his cheeks and came nowhere near his eyes.

"Hatteras." Tino nodded back with no smile on any part of his face.

Hatteras. I recalled the man as I heard the name. Montgomery Hatteras, the District Attorney. I'd heard Phillip (turn head and spit) rant about him. He was tough and ambitious. Cold hearted and charming. He could work the media like a master puppeteer. And he only got involved in high profile cases that he was sure were slam dunks.

I turned to Tino, hoping for a little reassurance that I wasn't going to be the one dunked in the slammer, but he was too busy having one of his canine face-offs with Hatteras. Did that man get along with anyone?

Hatteras closed the door and stepped up to the table, brushing aside McBeige as he did so. I watched the door close with a feeling of misgiving; there wasn't enough air even with it open. My breath came fast and choppy as I tried to compensate.

Hatteras turned his eyes on me and I felt a shaft of ice go down my spine. Cold and charming. When Phillip had said that, I'd wondered how someone can be both cold and charming at the same time. Now I knew.

"Ms. D'Angelo," he purred. "Let's all save ourselves the time and aggravation. We all know that you shot Lucienne Rudd. We have witnesses that place you at the scene of the crime. You know you had a motive that was so overwhelming that a jury could convict on that alone. And we have your confession. Let's talk a deal."

I opened my mouth to protest, but Mallory cut me off.

". It will only bolster our case when I shred it into Witnesses that have her leaving the scene of the crime nearly an hour before it happened. A confession so flimsy, so contrived and so dubious that I could only hope that you have the stupidity to introduce it in courtthe useless compost that it is. And if motive were enough to convict a criminal, you'd been doing twenty consecutive life sentences yourself. No deal, no talking. We demand a bail hearing."

My legs trembled and my eyes had trouble focusing. Did anyone else notice how little air there was? I've got closets bigger than this room. I pushed my chair back against the wall in effort to find some breathing space, but Hatteras, maybe thinking that I was retreating, leaned further in. His nose was within inches of mine. I felt like I was pinned against the wall. The oxygen count dropped drastically by the moment.

"Nobody will blame you, Josephine. We all know it's more than any woman could stand, seeing your fiancé cheat on you like that."

I wanted to tell him to call me Jo. I wanted to tell him that I hate the name Josephine. I wanted to tell him that the most drastic revenge that I had been planning on Phillip was wearing his favorite salmon-colored suit and never speaking to him again. But when I opened my mouth to speak, all that came out was…

"Uh-oh."

The room went blinding white and I slumped to the floor like a puddle of warm jello.

CHAPTER FOURTEEN

Do you know when you first wake up in a strange place and you don't know where you are for a moment?

No such luck for me.

The distant sound of voices bouncing off concrete walls woke me. The next thing I was aware of was the hard vinyl bench that I was lying on. And I knew exactly where I was.

Oh God. I'm in jail.

I rubbed my feet together. Hmm. No shoes, but still had nylons on. My fingers moved gingerly to feel my clothes. Wool-blend knit not canvas cotton-polyester. I was still in my Alfani suit, not a prison jumpsuit. It can't be that bad. Maybe I should open my eyes.

Let's not rush this.

As I lay motionless, I felt the presence of someone else in the room. Maybe it was in the way the sound echoed off one wall, yet was absorbed by the other part of the room. Maybe it was the dim scent of something spicy and familiar. Maybe garlic.

"C'mon, Joey. I know you're awake," said a deep, annoyingly familiar voice.

Joey? JOEY? Blearily, I opened one eye.

I was in another concrete block, closet-sized room. This one had pepto-bismol pink walls (which clashed horribly with my suit), the cot-like vinyl divan that I was lying on, an old upholstered chair (currently occupied by the innately aggravating Tino) and, thank God, a tall, very narrow window which was cranked open to allow in the refreshing aroma of car exhaust and dumpster fumes.

"The name is Jo, not Joey," I mumbled, "but you can call me Ms. D'Angelo."

Tino ignored my grouchiness and I ignored his chuckle as I swung my feet off the divan and pulled myself up to a sitting position. The room swayed giddily for a moment before settling back into this dimension.

"C'mon, let's go." Tino stood and extended his hand to help me up.

I stared at the proffered palm. "Huh? Go? Where?"

"Home. I think mine for the moment."

"What? Did I sleep through the bail hearing?"

"No. They've dropped the charges."

Damn, I'm good. Mental note: Write thesis about avoiding jail time by passing out during interrogation. We'll call it the D'Angelo Faint Feint.

"Why?" I was aiming for polite curiosity, but my voice went with paranoid skepticism.

His smile did a poor job of hiding some amusing secret as he pulled me to my feet and waited while I slipped my shoes back on.

"I'll let Julie tell you," he said as he led me out into the hall.

Julie???

CHAPTER FIFTEEN

Weakened as I was by stress and exhaustion, I allowed myself to be dragged back into the bedlam of the Scollari Spaghetti Circus.

It appeared as if I now had an assigned chair at the Scollari table. That worried me. Julie was already there, chatting at Uncle Luigi. I say "chatting at" because there was no indication that Uncle Luigi heard a word that she said. She turned when I came in and shot me a huge smile. I smiled back but something was doing pilates in my stomach. I knew that glitter in her eye and I knew fear. What had she been up to?

I sat down across from Auntie Lou who smiled warmly at me.

"Hello dearie! And who are you?"

Right. I thought hard about how to answer this.

"MY NAME IS JOSEPHINE," I said, slowly and loudly.

"What a nice name. Can I call you 'Jo'?"

Tino's and Julie's smirks were not helpful.

"THAT WOULD BE FINE."

She turned to Tino. "This one is much nicer than the one yesterday," she whispered loudly. Turning back to me she added, "And don't you worry about the whore that was floating around here. I'm sure that Tino has forgotten all about her already."

Maybe I could fix Auntie Lou up with Barry the security guard at work.

Mama Scollari took a rest from her marathon laps between the stove and the table to shoot a question at Stephanie.

"Stephanie, is there anything you want to tell us?"

From the tone of her voice, it was evident that she already knew what the news was. Stephanie looked over at me red-faced and rolled her eyes. Then she looked down at her daughter who sat between us.

"Today, Jenna went munty on the duck."

During the round of hearty applause and the chorus of *Good girl, Jenna* that followed this statement, I shot a look over to Julie. She grinned as if she understood what all this meant.

"I go munty on the duck like a big girl!" exclaimed Jenna, waving her spoon with pride.

A scrap of spaghetti arced over my head to land with a splat on Tino's plate. Without missing a beat, it got dragged into the heap to be included in the next mouthful. His fork paused.

"Toilet rather than diaper," he said, noticing my bewilderment.

"Oh."

"So Jo," asked Stephanie innocently. "What was your morning like?"

I paused, rudderless in the storm.

"Um, I can't top that." I said, gesturing toward Jenna.

Tino stepped in to fill the void. "Jo was falsely arrested this morning for murder, but in less than two hours, Julie found the evidence to prove her innocence."

Everyone stared at me, but I was too busy staring at Julie.

"You did? How?" Thank God that Julie isn't over-sensitive, because the degree of shock in my voice was not that flattering.

The panache acquired from five high school plays and eight community theater productions finally had a practical application as Julie gladly took center stage and recounted her morning.

CHAPTER SIXTEEN

"Well, this morning," Julie started, "I was having breakfast at the Dunkin Donuts…"

"What did you have?" asked Stephanie.

"A Big Gulp coffee and a chocolate crème donut." Julie didn't seem to think that this was as stupid a question as the rest of us did. Stephanie nodded in approval and Julie continued.

"Someone had left the Globe on one of the tables and Lucy Rudd's shooting was on the front page. It mentioned that the police were looking for Jo in connection with the murder…"

"Did it actually mention me by name?" I asked, horrified.

Julie nodded. "So I tried to call you. There was no answer at the house or your office and your cellphone was turned off."

"Why did you turn off your cellphone?" Tino watched me closely as he asked.

"I didn't want to talk to Phillip." I answered, not meeting his eyes. "He kept trying to call me last night and I didn't want to hear it."

"Good call." Julie nodded in approval.

Tino shot a sharp glance at Julie.

"You don't know Phillip." She answered his

unasked question. "He's a lawyer. By the time he was done explaining what had happened, He'd have Jo believing it was all her fault. I've seen him do it before."

I looked down into my dinner, trying to hide my face. It was true, though. I had never actually caught him cheating on me, but I had always let him talk me out of suspecting him. And it had always been easier to blame myself then to argue with him.

"So then I called Tino and since he asked me, so politely, if I would come into the office, I dropped everything and drove over here." Julie shot Tino one of her teasing looks and I could tell from his twisted smirk that, rather than a polite request, he had probably barked an order at her.

"You dropped everything?" asked Stephanie. "What about the donut?"

"Casualty of war." Julie replied. "Got left on the table."

Stephanie was devastated.

"Not to minimize the importance of chocolate crème donuts," I snapped, "but can we please get back to the story?"

"I got to the office just as you called in. Tino went to the Police Station and sent me down to the house in Cohasset to look for clues."

"*Look for clues?*" Tino shook his head in dismay. "You make it sound like a Nancy Drew adventure. What I asked was that you get down there before they could get the search warrant issued. I just wanted someone from our side on the premises so that no exonerating evidence got 'accidentally' overlooked or misplaced by the police."

Julie airily waved away Tino's correction.

"It took nearly an hour to get down to Cohasset. The traffic was crawling like an algebra class. By the time I pulled into the driveway, there was a cop already posted outside. Fortunately, he was both young and cute so it took me all of about twenty seconds to get past him and into the house.

"Ant Bee was still out. Her Saab wasn't in the garage, the breakfast dishes were still on the table, and I saw the note she had left, so I figured she hadn't been in all morning. She probably didn't even know what was going on yet.

"The house was pretty much as it always is, neat and clean, except Jo's bedroom."

I made a noise to try to interrupt her. I didn't want her to announce to the entire table what a mess my bedroom was, but she was on a roll and there was no stopping her. She plowed on.

"The suit Jo had worn yesterday was still draped over a chair. I sniffed the cuffs, there was no smell of gunpowder on them, which was good. I was sure it would test negative for gun residue."

"You can recognize the smell of gunpowder?" Stephanie was impressed.

Julie rolled her eyes. "Dad and Jo used to always go out shooting. As soon as I'd walked into the house, I could tell if they'd been out to the firing range."

Tino looked over at me, his face was very hard to read, but I thought his glance held a touch of suspicion. I ignored it and Julie continued.

"I went through the rest of the house and couldn't find anything interesting. It wasn't until I went out to the deck that I caught my big break.

"That," Julie told her pasta-saturated audience, "is where I found the remains of the chocolate ice cream that had dripped on to the table and then on to the deck. It had to have happened the prior night, since Ant Bee hadn't found it yet to clean it up."

I grimaced. I hadn't even thought that Ant Bee would have to clean up the ice cream drippings on the deck. If I had thought about it at all, I just figured that it would get washed away by the next rain.

"And chocolate ice cream drippings are evidence of... what?" besides Josephine D'Angelo's stupidity and thoughtlessness.

"I found the box in the trash," Julie beamed.

"And..."

"It was Ben and Jerry's Chocolate Fudge Brownie!" she crowed triumphantly.

I looked around. Thank God. Everyone else looked as befuddled as I felt.

"Ant Bee won't buy Ben and Jerry's ice cream," Julie explained to Mama Scollari. "She thinks that they're pinko commie Nazis."

This was true, but don't go thinking that Ant Bee is a bigot. She hates everyone. She thinks that democrats are commies and republicans are fascists and the schools in America are nowhere near as good as they are in Hungary. Sometimes I wondered why she's still here.

"So I knew," Julie continued, "that Jo had to have bought the ice cream herself. I couldn't find the receipt, but the bag was from Cumberland Farms. So I drove over to the Cumberland Farms down on Endicott Street. Danny was behind the counter, he told me that A.J. had been the clerk on the night before, so while Danny was pulling the surveillance video and the register receipts, I called A.J.'s cell phone…"

"How did you get the cell phone number of the night clerk at the Cumberland Farms?" Tino asked the question that everyone was thinking.

"He gave it to me. We went out on a date once. Oh, and Jo," Julie turned back to me, "A.J. says that if you're going to dump your old boyfriend, he wants me to tell you that he's available and he thinks you're hot."

"Nice to know." I said faintly, "I'll keep that in mind."

"So, then I took the video tape with the cash register printouts to the police station." Julie dropped her voice into her Joe Friday imitation. "According to the evidence, at 8:52 last night, Josephine D'Angelo drove up to the Cumberland Farms on Endicott Street in Cohasset. At 8:54 she used her bank card to purchase a half gallon of ice cream and left immediately thereafter. By the way, Detective McAdams checked your bank records, which supported the fact that you could not have been thirty miles away in Dorchester four minutes later when Lucy Rudd was shot. Case closed!"

An awed hush followed this statement. Julie bowed her head in mock humility as she accepted the applause that the silence implied.

"Wow," I said finally. "I'm impressed."

Julie's eyes glowed. "I told you Jo! I'm good at this!"

"Wow," I said again. "Are you telling me you abandoned a chocolate crème filled donut? For me?"

Julie's face reflected the gravity of this issue. "Yes, it was a sacrifice, but you <u>are</u> my only sister."

My head dropped in humility. "I'm not worthy." I sighed.

"True. But just wait until you get my bill."

The Scollaris had been listening to our banter with amusement and no little awe, except for Auntie Lou who surprisingly, seemed to have followed the gist of our conversation.

"Hmm. Then if it wasn't the commie, then who did kill the slut?"

CHAPTER SEVENTEEN

"What part of 'it wasn't me' aren't you understanding?"

My teeth were grinding as I stood in the office of my boss, Frank Bishop, trying real hard not to dive off into a psycho rant.

"I understand." Frank was doing his kindly Uncle Count Olaf imitation. "But there's been a lot of publicity over this and the partners feel that a little time off might be in order. Just to give you some space to recuperate."

"Space, my ass! And don't give me that crap about 'the partners'. This is your call because you don't think this jives with your 'corporate image'."

Has anyone ever seen Sauron smile? I'm betting he looks a lot like Frank Bishop faking patient benevolence.

I turned and walked out the door without another word.

❦

A strange car sat parked in the driveway of the Cohasset house. I maneuvered my Lexus around it and made it in to the garage, but stepped back out into the driveway to investigate.

Detective McBeige hadn't been leaning against the car when I pulled in, but like some sit-com wizard, he was lounging casually against its door when I strode back out. I glanced up, looking for whatever tree or helicopter he might have dropped out of. On his face, a ghost of a smile was promptly exorcised as he straightened and turned to me.

"We need to talk."

I looked at him suspiciously. His entire demeanor was different from our last two conversations. This wasn't the unobtrusive yet devious spectator that I met in Phillip's office. And it wasn't the hard-nosed interrogator who drilled me at the police station. While I was far from trusting him, I was curious.

"Are you still looking for evidence to convict me?" I crossed my arms over my chest.

"No," he eyed me carefully, "but I am still investigating the murder of Lucy Rudd and there may be a connection to you."

I studied him for a moment before inviting him in with a twitch of my head. I opened the gate, headed up the stairs to the back deck and entered through the French doors that led to the sunroom.

"Hi, Ant Bee! It's just me, Jo!" I announced loudly. "And I've brought a guest."

"Sot?" Ant Bee's bark preceded her into the sunroom as she waddled out from the kitchen. "If you have brought a guest, zen it is not just you!"

I have no idea what 'sot' means, but I'm

guessing she's calling me names.

She stood in the doorway, her arms akimbo, a squat grey fire hydrant of domestic surliness. She glared at Detective McBeige for such a long moment that he began to sweat.

"Coffee. Arabian. Black. Three sugars." Her voice rang like some medieval mystic proclaiming Armageddon.

In McBeige's eyes, I could see a flicker of fear tussle with the anticipation of getting a fresh cup of coffee, just the way he liked it. He nodded mutely.

"Water." She eyed me with disgust. "From a bottle." She spat out the words, making it sound like I wanted a glass of blood from sacrificed babies.

"And don't give me one of the used bottles filled with tap water!" I called after her as she muttered back into the kitchen.

I gestured for McBeige to sit in one of the overstuffed chairs and I plopped down in to another. The sunroom was one of the least daunting rooms in the house. I had thought about speaking to him in the formal dining room or, even better, Dad's wood paneled study, but to say the truth, I was more comfortable in the sunroom and I was having a tough enough day already without freaking myself out by blowing my home court advantage. I kicked off my shoes, curled my feet underneath me, rested my chin on the oversized pillow that I hugged to my chest, and waited for McBeige to speak.

He squirmed uncomfortably in the silence,

trying to sit in a chair that was designed for comfort, not for authority. I hid my grin with the top of the pillow as he maneuvered himself to balance on the rim of the seat, abandoning the rest of the chair as a bad bet.

He opened his mouth several times, but nothing came out. I could tell he didn't know where to start and after the crap he had put me through that morning, I wasn't feeling very helpful. In fact, I was kind of enjoying having the tables turned.

A short reprieve was granted in the form of Ant Bee, re-entering with refreshments. She placed his coffee and a plate of bland dry biscuits on the end table. She smiled broadly at McBeige, a sight which is actually much more unsettling than her scowl. He nodded a thank you as he reached for his cup.

A glass of ice with an open bottle of water was placed just out of my reach. I leaned forward, grabbed the bottle and took a small sip. I stifled a sigh. Why do I bother? Tap water again. Ant Bee had an ethical opposition to spending money on something that came out of the faucet for free.

"Ms. D'Angelo," McBeige dived in. "On behalf of the department, I'd like to offer you an apology for the misunderstanding this morning."

I was in the middle of swallowing a large mouthful of water and an unladylike snort caused a fountain of water to squirt form my nose. I glared at him speechlessly. Misunderstanding?

He looked a little sheepish as he handed me a napkin. I watched him closely as I wiped up the mess. I didn't think that he was here to incriminate me, but I didn't think he had driven all the way out to Cohasset to apologize either.

He was a bit of a chameleon, changing from one animal to another without warning. At Phillip's office, I had seen him as a toad, hunched benignly in the corner, waiting to snag an unsuspecting insect with his deceptive tongue. At the police station, he had been a feral cat, toying with me, prodding me with his verbal claws. Later, in the interrogation room, he seemed like no more than a vulture, a carrion picker, waiting for his chance after the bigger predators were done with me.

But at the moment he looked like nothing more than a puzzled sheep dog, worried about something that I couldn't see.

"I need to ask you something," he continued. "How do you know Tino Scollari?"

That question surprised me and I didn't know how to answer him. I felt no great desire to open up to him, but I couldn't see any purpose in lying to him either.

"My sister worked with him on a case recently. She's thinking about working with him full time in the future."

There. That was ambiguous enough without lying. Though God only knew what "working with him" might entail or lead to.

"You're a wealthy woman, Ms. D'Angelo?" It wasn't really a question. I didn't know where he was going with this and I got the feeling that he didn't know how to get there.

"Lucky for me, since your little 'misunderstanding' this morning just cost me my job." I didn't bother masking my bitterness on that one.

He looked guilty, as he should. "The department, of course, will issue a press release acknowledging your innocence."

Yeah, and it will run on page C-9 of the Herald, right after the obituary notices.

He stood up and began to pace the room. I held my tongue, more than a little puzzled, and waited.

"What do you know about Tino Scollari?"

That question held me speechless for a moment. What do I say? He's big? He's aggravating? He smells good? His family is insane? His mother makes a damn good spaghetti sauce?

When in doubt, answer a question with a question.

"What do *you* know about Tino Scollari?" I shot back.

Evidently, that was the twenty-two dollar question.

"About eight years ago, Scollari was on the Boston Police force, a patrol officer trying to make detective, when he and his partner stumbled onto a Kokkinos hit."

My fingers suddenly felt stiff and chilled. I tucked them under my armpits. I had heard of the Kokkinos. Supposedly, it was an old Greek fraternal organization, the "Kokkinos Cheri", the Red Hand.

Yet in the past couple of decades, there had been growing reports that it was actually an organized crime syndicate with roots that went back to the middle ages. Unlike their Italian cousins, the Mafia, the Kokkinos had kept a very low profile. In recent years however, they'd been getting a lot of press, taking the blame, or the credit, for some very flashy crimes and some very gory murders.

And the Kokkinos were known to have little respect and no fear of the law.

"It was the break the D.A. was looking for. The killer, Niko Mavros, was very highly placed in the brotherhood, actually the nephew to the Gerosandres."

"Geros… ?" It wasn't a word that I'd ever heard before.

"Gerosandres. The head of the Kokkinos. Literally, it means 'the Old One' or 'the Old Man'. Hatteras was sure that Niko would turn if he could make a strong case. Unfortunately, Niko made bail and within 24 hours, Scollari's partner, Steve Beck, was found in his car, parked by the Fens, a bullet buried in his forehead."

I wondered where all my blood went. I felt ice cold from head to toe. I vaguely remembered that murder and the pandemonium that followed. And Scollari had been in the middle of all that?

"Hatteras ordered Scollari into a safe house, but Scollari broke out and the next day, Niko was found dead. Ballistics tied the bullet to Scollari's gun, but Scollari had an alibi. Besides, you weren't going to find a jury who was going to convict a decorated ex-marine turned cop who *may* have shot his partner's murderer. Hatteras couldn't even get a judge to indict him. It never went to trial, and Scollari was 'allowed' to resign from the police force."

In the silence that followed all I could hear was the rumble of the waves against the rocks and pulsing of the grandfather clock in the foyer.

"Why are you telling me all this?" My voice didn't sound much louder than the surf outside.

McBeige stood up and walked to the French doors.

"I've been a cop for seventeen years, and a homicide detective for nine of them. I've seen a lot of dead bodies in that time, and met almost as many killers. And, I have to tell you, there are a few things that I've learned." He turned and looked at me. "When a person kills in self-defense, it changes you. Nothing you can do about it, it was either him or you, but either way, you lose a little corner of your soul. You work at it, pray if it helps, but it's always there, like a bubble of acid in the back of your brain. But you survive."

There was a haunted gleam lurking in his eyes that made me think he was speaking of himself.

"But when a man goes out hunts down another human being and kills him in cold blood, no matter how powerful the reason, he's crossed the line."

McBeige walked back and sat down in front of me, leaning in close and staring into my eyes. "That's why we can't let killers go free. Not for revenge, not to pacify the masses, and not to set an example for the rest of society. But because when a person has intentionally murdered another human being, he's gone too far. He's crossed that line and killing is no longer taboo. It's just a means to an end. Maybe it's a last resort, but it's still an option, and, if the need is great enough, he will kill again."

He finished the coffee in one long gulp, slipped a few of the biscuits into his coat pocket, and stood up.

"Call me. Anytime. For any reason." He dropped his business card on the coffee table and headed for the door, not pausing as he called into the kitchen. "Excellent coffee, Ant Bee. Thanks very much."

I heard the door open and close, but I didn't see him go. I stared blindly at his card, my mind still hearing all the words he had said.

I picked up the card and slid it into my pocket.

CHAPTER EIGHTEEN

You would think that with the way my week had been going, Thursday could only get better and yet there was no telling my body that.

Inches from my head, the alarm clock glowed 10:47 AM. I had long since outlasted the snooze bar and I was now lying, comatose, my eyeballs drying out from gazing unblinkingly at the ceiling.

I should be at work, but I didn't have a job. If this were a normal day off, I would be with my fiancé, but I didn't have a fiancé. I could take the dog for a walk on the beach, but I didn't have a dog.

I laid there for another hour or so, wondering how I suddenly could have absolutely no life at all. I rolled over and stared at the alarm clock.

10:48. I think I was stuck in a time wrinkle. Maybe aliens had abducted me and then brought me back to the same minute that they had snatched me from. Maybe I should get out of bed.

Let's not rush this.

The faint ringing of a phone from somewhere in the bowels of the house intruded on my pity party. The way my week was going, it could only be bad news. I pulled my blankets over my head.

"Sot?" I could hear Ant Bee chugging her way up stairs, talking loudly on the portable phone. "Oh, no. Little princess is not out of bed yet. Oh, no. Little princess knows zat I don't mind waiting all day to make ze beds. Hokay, I see if she can squash you into her busy schedule."

I added two pillows to the layers covering my head but it was like a paper parasol in a hurricane. The bedroom door banged open.

"Wake up! Wake up and smell ze telephone!"

Hands pulled at pillows and the quilt disappeared like the ebbing tide. I groaned, rolled over, and buried my face in the mattress, to no avail.

"Up, up, up! You have a telephone call!"

"Mzpfz gjdz dzd?" Roughly translated: "Who is it?"

"It is Rhonda from your office."

I could feel the phone being wedged between my cheek and the mattress. Maybe I should answer the phone.

"Hi Rhonda." Even to my own ears, my voice sounded scratchy.

"You okay?"

"I'll live." I pushed myself up to a sitting position and rubbed my hand over my eyes and up into my hair. "What's happening in the real world?"

"Couldn't tell ya, but here at Chandler, Chandler and Bishop, the feces have struck the oscillating ventilator."

"Why? What's happening?"

"I spent most of the morning taking calls from clients who had seen the news and were calling to see how you were doing. I told them the truth, that you had been put on 'administrative leave' even though the police had dropped the charges."

I snorted into the phone. "I take it that long term job security is not one of your career objectives."

"Screw this place."

I was finding it hard to argue with that line of thinking.

"I'm cleaning out my desk now. I figure I'll come work for you when you open your own office."

That woke me up. "My own what?"

"Well, since Bishop is refusing to service the pro bono job you took on for Scollari, you'll need to set up your own shingle to handle that one, and since most of the calls I've had this morning have left messages asking that you let them know when you open your own office, I figure that it won't be long before you'll need a legal assistant."

Okay, this was frightening. The idea of opening my own law office was only slightly less scary than becoming a private investigator with Julie.

"Um, Rhonda, I don't know if—"

"Oops, gotta go. Security is here to escort me out of the building." I heard some familiar voices in the background. "Oh. Marcia says 'hi'. And I'll be by this afternoon to drop off the Scollari files."

"But--"

She hung up abruptly and I was left staring blindly at a dead receiver.

Maybe I should get out of bed.

CHAPTER NINETEEN

The large box landed with a disturbingly weighty thud on the dining room table. Behind it stood Rhonda, her hands on her hip looking like she was waiting for entrance applause. For the occasion, she had dressed casual. She was still in animal print mode, but today she wore a tight leopard print leisure suit with a tiger claw necklace. Very primordial.

"What's this?" I asked as I wrestled off the lid.

"O'Halloran's response." Her face was deceptively neutral.

"All this?" I was horrified. It had to be five thousand pages. He must have had a platoon of legal temps working all night.

"This is just box one of three." Rhonda twitched with glee. "You should have seen Bishop's face when the courier dropped them off."

"O'Halloran's insane!" I said, picking up the first stack and paging through it. "All he's going to do is piss off the judge if tries to enter all these into evidence."

Rhonda sniffed. She didn't have to say what we both knew, that he had no intention of submitting the responses, he was just trying to bury the opposition in paperwork.

I reached for my laptop and grabbed the first file. My dander was raised; the call to battle rang in my ears.

"Go get the rest of the files. We're going to be working late tonight."

Rhonda headed for the door but I could hear her bark of laughter as I muttered to myself.

"Stand your ground," I mumbled, booting up the computer. "Do not fire unless fired upon, but if they mean to have a war, let it start here."

CHAPTER TWENTY

By three a.m., Rhonda was a lifeless drumlin of faux-fur, sprawled across the sofa, her snores drowning out the roar of the surf from outside. Even Ant Bee's extra strong Arabian coffee couldn't hold back that tide.

Ant Bee had retired hours ago, muttering in Hungarian, probably placing some gypsy cabal curse on us all as she tottered off to bed, but not before making a gallon or so of thick, black java.

I, however, had kicked into hyper-drive. The adrenalin that carried me through finals at law school returned as I plowed through responses and interrogatories. I was in the zone and I wasn't stopping until I had served each and every volley back into O'Halloran's court. I chugged a mouthful of lukewarm liquid caffeine and grabbed the next file.

The sharp buzz of my cell phone sounded like a fire alarm amidst the rhythmic rattle of Rhonda's snoring and the muffling surf. I grabbed for it quickly but I didn't need to worry; it would probably take a tsunami to wake her, or perhaps the presence of just one relatively good looking male.

I didn't recognize the number on the phone, but

it had a Boston area code. I walked over to French doors before answering it.

"Hello?" I whispered, not wanting to wake Rhonda.

"Jo?" A familiarly gruff voice asked.

"Tino? What are you doing calling at this hour?"

"I'm outside your house and I could see that you're still up."

"What are you doing outside my house?" If my voice was a slightly ruder than normal, well pardon me, I was a little freaked out. McBeige's warning was still fresh in my mind and the jury was still out as to whether I believed Scollari capable of murder or not.

"I've been on surveillance outside your house. There's something about Lucy's murder that's bothering me. We need to talk."

The idea that Scollari had been staking out my house all night only added to the twilight zone aura that had been shadowing me all week. I glanced over at Rhonda, still wheezing somnolently on the couch.

"Okay, come in through the side gate and up the stairs to the deck, I'll let you in through the French doors." No way was I going to meet him alone in the driveway.

In the stark moonlight, his shadow reached the door before he did. I had unlatched the door and I now stood back behind the dining room table, unsure if I should be cursing myself for being so wary of him, or cursing myself for being so stupid as to let him in.

Both doors swung in and he stood silhouetted on the threshold, a huge dark outline looming featureless against the bright night sky. My fingers trembled as I pressed my palms against the back of the chair.

I had had way too much coffee. I was wired, dizzy like I was drunk, but unlike alcohol, which made me sleepy, I was tense and alert.

He stepped into the room and as the light hit his face, I could see that annoying smirk. He raised an eyebrow at me before glancing around the room, taking in the systematic chaos of my "home office".

"What's all this?" he asked, picking up one of the several dozen folders that were stacked and strewn all over the dining room.

"We've been working on the O'Halloran litigation."

That tone of martyrdom comes naturally to us Catholic girls. Go ahead, it implies, you go on and have fun on your stake out while we slave away all night, typing our fingers to the bone on legal responses. Don't think about us, we're not important…

Catholic guilt doesn't always work that well on some men, but Tino responded quite satisfactorily, squirming uncomfortably and clearing his throat several times before being able to speak again.

"Is this the, um, normal amount of paperwork for a situation like this?"

I thought about what would be the best way to respond. Would it make him feel guiltier if I told him the truth, that this was a ridiculous amount of discovery with the only motive being bureaucratic harassment? Or maybe I should tell him that this was the typical workload for a suit like this.

I compromised with an eloquent shrug and sat back down in front of my laptop. I picked up a file and looked at it blindly, watching him from the corner of my eye as he glanced at the ostensible corpse on the sofa, as well as the rest of the disarray.

"Did you have friends over tonight?" he asked, puzzled.

"Just Rhonda and I."

His glance took in the dozen or so coffee cups that were scattered all over the room. Another half a dozen clean mugs were still lined up next to the coffee urn that Ant Bee had left out.

"Oh," I said, perceiving his confusion. "I don't like using a dirty cup."

I am not weird. Or at least I'm not neurotic. It's just the idea of refilling a dirty cup is, um, icky. Tino gave a snort of amusement which I chose to ignore.

"I've been doing some follow up on the Rudd murder and--"

"Why?" I watched him warily. "Did someone hire you? Did the police ask for your help?"

I did feel a small pang of remorse as his face twitched from the sting of my words. I'd guess that the police had *not* asked for his help and it was a little bit of a sore spot.

"The police have come up with nothing so far for suspects." Scollari chose to ignore my interruption. "Lucienne Rudd had a very boring life. Few friends and even less family, it appears the only thing that she had besides her job were the sporadic little encounters with Gorson."

I didn't want to hear this. I stood up abruptly and began clearing away empty coffee mugs. When I got six of them dangling from my fingers, I retreated into the kitchen. Scollari said nothing and when I returned to the dining room, he was sitting at the table, watching me expressionlessly.

"Maybe it was just a drive-by." I offered. "You know, random gang-related violence."

"She was shot six times at a range of between twenty and twenty-five feet. She was just getting into her car when she was killed."

I was silent while I took another load of coffee cups into the kitchen.

Six shots. Could be a semi-automatic, but if someone were to shoot six times, chances were they were emptying the cylinder. Probably a revolver. That also reduced the possibility of a random shooting. Six shots is a pretty decisive statement. Somebody really wanted her dead. And to connect all six bullets at a range of over twenty feet meant the shooter was a fairly good shot, a person familiar with guns.

I grabbed a clean coffee cup, filled it and poured my normal golfball of sugar into the sludge. I jerked my head to offer Scollari a mug. He accepted with an equally wordless reply but waived off the sugar. I bit back a smile as I sipped the brew. Scollari was going to try to drink Ant Bee's coffee black. No sugar.

I watched as his eyes watered. Impressive. No noticeable flinching, but he did turn about six shades redder. His hand shook as he placed the mug back down on the table. I reached over to pour about an inch of sugar into his cup.

"Don't think of it as coffee. It helps." I offered.

"Were you planning on sleeping at all this week?"

"Well, as Ant Bee says, 'A wet bird never flies at night.'"

Scollari was back to his deer-in-the-headlights look as he thought that one over.

"What the hell does that mean?" he asked finally.

"It helps if you don't think of it as logic."

A hush settled on the room. I stared into my coffee mug, my eyes watching the thick fluid clinging to the sides of the mug. I chewed on my lip, biting back the questions that my mind really wanted to ask.

My teeth lost.

"And what was Phillip doing all this time? Before maligning me to the police, I mean."

Boy, did that came out a lot more bitter than I planned.

"He was questioned. He said he was still up in his condo on his phone. He came up clean on the gunpowder residue test. And witnesses have him leaving his apartment and getting to the crime scene a minute or two after the shots were fired."

I pushed the papers on the table into piles, using my fingernail to line up the edges into razor edge precision. I didn't think I wanted to hear more, but I wasn't quite ready to change the subject either.

"First officer on the scene stated that Gorson was sitting on the curb, with his head in his hands. The report indicated that Gorson was mumbling 'Why, Joe? Why? How could you do this?' Under further questioning, he admitted that he was referring to his fiancée, whom he suspected of shooting his secretary."

"Yeah right, 'secretary'," I snorted.

I could feel Tino staring me, though my eyes were locked on my coffee cup. The dregs of the coffee swished lethargically as I swirled it. I stared at the residue, wishing I could read them like tea leaves.

Like a snapped twig, I slapped the cup down onto the table and stood up suddenly. I strode fiercely around the room, my arms wrapped tightly across my chest.

"Can you believe the ego of that guy?" I exploded. "He actually thinks that he is such a prize that I would kill someone over him! That self-absorbed, self-centered, arrogant prig!"

I had this huge urge to throw a chair through a window. I compromised and kicked the coffee table. Hard. My toes would have preferred that I had sacrificed the window.

I plopped ungracefully onto the sofa, jostling Rhonda. She groaned faintly and pulled one of the toss pillows over her head. Rhonda lives next to the T-tracks in Revere. Gunshots, fired within six feet of her head, would probably be the only thing that could wake her. I rubbed my toes and glared at Tino.

"Why are you telling me this?"

Déjà vu. I had asked McBeige the same question when he told me about Tino's past.

Tino was blunt where McBeige was ambiguous, but they both carried the same message.

"I don't think that Lucy Rudd was the intended victim."

I waved him to silence. I didn't want him to continue. But he didn't need to. The possibility had been treading water in the quagmire of my brain for hours and I had been stalwartly ignoring its splashes.

A woman with my color hair (almost) came out of my fiancé's house, walked to a car that looked very similar to mine and was shot and killed. The fact that Lucy Rudd's compulsion to imitate me might have been the cause of her murder was a statement I didn't want anyone to make. And yet there it was, lurking in the backwaters of my mind.

Duck and cover. Here it comes. Catholic Guilt. Don't waste your breath on logic, I knew it wasn't my fault, and yet I was going to have to do one hell of a lot of rosaries before I got over this one.

I postponed my hair shirt atonement appointment for a later date. There was a far more burning question that needed answering.

"But why would anyone want to kill *me*?"

"That's what we need to find out."

CHAPTER TWENTY-ONE

The French doors closed with a reassuring click. I stood, my forehead leaning against the cool glass while I listened to Tino's steps fading as he descended the stairs. Obedient to my instructions, I turned the dead bolt on the doors but it was a lame concession to security; if anyone wanted to break in, the large panes of glass would slow them down less than a door knob.

I turned and immediately bit back a scream. A grotesque parody of a head was resting on the back of the sofa, grinning at me.

"Damn, woman! You got hotties coming out of the woodwork! I'm calling first dibs on your sloppy seconds!"

Evidently I was correct in my assumption that it would take either gunshots or a warm male body to wake Rhonda. Her bright yellow hair was disheveled and stood up on end like a crop of mini bananas. Her mascara had run down her cheeks and she looked like a rabid raccoon made up like a harlequin doll. Frightening.

"Please, don't wait for me." I tossed my head to point to the door where Tino had exited. "Go right ahead and knock yourself out."

I handed Rhonda a napkin so that she could wipe off the mascara.

"Question. If you die, who gets the money?"

"I thought you were sleeping." I needed another cup of coffee.

"You weren't exactly whispering. Who gets the money?"

I sighed. She was not going to be diverted. I crumbled.

"Julie. Right now all the assets are in trust funds with just the two of us as beneficiaries. Uncle Benny and I control the Trusts. Over the next six years, the trusts will be dissolved and the assets will be divided, fifty-fifty. If either of us dies before then, the remaining beneficiary gets everything."

"So it must be Julie who's trying to kill you!"

The idea was so ridiculous that I snorted a laugh. "You don't know my sister very well. I doubt there's a less mercenary human being on the planet. When we were kids, she'd have given away her entire week's lunch money before we'd even caught the Monday morning bus. She's a soft touch for every bum and beggar she comes across. The main reason for my father establishing the trusts was to prevent her from throwing away her half of the estate. I'm hoping she'll eventually get married to someone with some common sense about money because I'm betting that when she finally gets control of her half of the estate, she'll end up giving it all away within a year."

"So who's on her list of favorite charities?"

"Let's go with the shorter list, who *isn't*?"

I buried my nose into a file. Rhonda, taking the hint that sharing time was over, curled back up on the sofa and was snoring stridently within minutes.

Which left me alone with only my suspicions for company. If I had been the intended victim, and the motive was to give my malleable sister control of her trust fund, then chances were I knew the murderer.

As I plowed through the O'Halloran responses, I began to create a mental list in the back of mind, adding and scratching names, expanding and willowing the roster of potential murderers, all the time avoiding the one skulking question that lingered.

If Lucy Rudd's murder had been a mistake and I had been the intended victim, would the killer try again? And if so, when?

CHAPTER TWENTY-TWO

I stumbled into my bedroom and collapsed on my bed still in the same sweatsuit that I had been wearing for the last twenty four hours. I was too tired to care. Sleep came quickly, but one last thought made me smirk into my pillow.

I would love to be a fly on the wall when O'Halloran took delivery of all my responses and counter-disclosures.

CHAPTER TWENTY-THREE

It was dark when I finally woke. A late nor'easter was pounding the house. The windows rattled and the wind groaned. A flare of lightning was followed quickly by a bone throbbing rumble of thunder. The muted staccato of a torrential rain was quickly building towards a climatic meteorological crescendo. I stretched like a cat, a contented mew escaping my throat.

I love thunderstorms. Someone had thrown a quilt over me while I slept and I curled it around me like a pastel cocoon. I snuggled into the pillows and listened to the roar of the sky vying with the wail of the ocean.

When we kids, Julie would make excuses to come to my bedroom whenever there was a thunderstorm. It's funny, because I was the one afraid of everything, but I liked storms, and Julie was the fearless one, except for that she hated thunder and lightning.

"Wanna play Monopoly?"

I laughed out loud as I rolled over to face the door. Julie stood on the threshold, the hall light shining behind her, a battered Monopoly set under one arm. I squirmed to a sitting position, crossing my legs underneath me and rubbing the last bit of sleep out of my eyes.

"You are a glutton for punishment." I always trashed Julie's butt when we played Monopoly. Anything that required strength, coordination, speed or grace, Julie aced me without sweating, but when it came to Monopoly, I ruled.

Julie leapt onto the bed, thumping up and down a couple of times for good measure before tossing the quilt to the floor and smoothing down the sheets to make a playing area.

"So what are you doing here?" I asked as I dealt out the money. (I'm always the banker.)

"I'm on a stake out."

"Stake out?"

"You know, surveillance."

"What are you surveilling?"

"You."

I snorted. "Let me know if I do anything interesting."

"Okay."

Julie smushed all her bills into a pile and pinned the wad under one cheek of her butt. I lined up my bills neatly under the edge of the board, no stacks touching. I set the iron on Go as Julie set out the Community Chest and Chance cards. She slid the Scotty dog over next to my iron and rolled the dice.

"Tino ask you to surveillancize me?"

"Uh-huh, but I don't know if surveillancize is a word."

"Did you understand what I meant?"

"Uh-huh." Julie acknowledged.

"Then it's a word."

"I'll make sure it gets into the next edition of the Funky Wagtail dictionary."

"You do that."

We didn't talk much for a bit, but it wasn't that quiet, what with the rain and the waves and the wind. A crack of lightning made Julie jump.

"You think it's necessary?" I asked.

"What? Lightling?"

I smiled at her childhood mispronunciation.

"No, not 'lightling'. Keeping an eye on me."

"Well, it's a bit weird, but someone did kill Lucy Rudd and I'm still kind of new to this detective thing so I figure its good training."

"I thought private detectives were supposed to sit in dark cars and chain smoke and pee into coffee cans." I said.

"Yeah, well, have you ever tried to pee into a can while sitting behind the wheel of a Miata MX-5? I can barely change out my nylons in that thing."

"I don't want to hear it."

I still have nightmares about the time we were speeding up Route 95, going about eighty miles an hour with Julie behind the wheel, when I realized that she had turned on the cruise control and was squirming out of her nylons to change into her jeans.

Julie bought Illinois Avenue, but I wasn't worried, I knew I could get it from her later. I passed on the B&O, saving my cash for the greens and the blues.

"When did you get here?" I glanced at my alarm clock. 8:42 pm. I had slept almost ten hours.

"I relieved Tino a little after one."

"This afternoon? Tino had been outside all night?"

"Uh-huh."

Whoa. I was having a Rod Serling moment. The idea that Tino had been sitting in his car outside my house all night and all morning was a bit weird. I had been much too tired when I had said goodbye to Rhonda and the Responses to pay much attention to what else might be parked on the street, but I did recall an old dark blue Lincoln Towncar parked up the street a ways. I remember wondering if the Van Hoovens might have had more visitors than their driveway could hold.

I really wasn't sure how that information made me feel, so I decided to file it in the back of my head for the moment and jump to the next question.

"You've been sitting out in your car since one this afternoon?"

"Well, no." Julie looked a bit sheepish. "While I am fully prepared to do a full shift of surveillance in my car if needed, I figured why bother watching from the outside when I could be sitting inside and, um, surveillancizing you from the kitchen. I've been downstairs talking with Ant Bee all afternoon."

"Fun. I'd rather sit out in the car."

"Actually it was. Ant Bee has been teaching me swear words in Hungarian."

"Now there's a skill that every résumé screams for."

"*Fakanal!*" said Julie.

"Excuse me?"

"*Fakanal!* It means 'wooden spoon'."

"Don't let Sister Benignus hear you talk like that," I told her, handing her the dice.

"Seven! I've got Boardwalk!" Julie's screech could ground bats.

I slapped my arms over the playing board, anchoring the pieces as best I could.

"On the floor! Don't do the Boardwalk dance on the bed!"

Julie's leap from the bed sent all the game pieces flying. She executed the obligatory Boardwalk Dance around the bedroom while I put the game board back together again.

Julie's victory was short-lived. An hour and forty five minutes later, she admitted defeat. She had managed to hang on to Boardwalk and Park Place to the bitter end, but I ended up with the rest of the board.

"Why won't you put more than one house on your properties? You've got to maximize your revenue."

"I just don't think it's fair to charge that much. Besides, I like my houses spread out, you know, a little bit of a lawn around them, some space in the backyard for a swingset." She put the cards and the small pieces back into the box while I organized the money. "How much do I owe you?"

"Seventeen thousand, four hundred and fifty."

"And that makes... ?"

I did the math in my head. "You're up to nine hundred, eleven thousand, six hundred and ten."

"Okay, let's make it an even million. We'll square when we settle the trust."

This had been the running joke since we were kids, but suddenly Lucy Rudd's murder and Rhonda's remarks made this all slightly un-funny.

"You know that we're kidding, don't you?" I asked, staring at her intently. "You do know that this is pretend money and that Daddy's trust fund is real money."

Julie shot me that secret little smile of hers that men find so adorable but which I just find frightening.

"Oh, *fakanal!*" I muttered under my breath.

CHAPTER TWENTY-FOUR

It was three o'clock in the morning and my body clock was on Tahiti Time. The storm had blown itself out but the moon was still hidden behind the clouds. Looking out over the beach, I paced the deck restlessly.

Upstairs, Julie was sprawled across my bed, dead to the world, hugging my Pummie. Pummie is a stuffed cat that was once purple and furry, but is now bald and grey.

Whatever aspirations she had to being a detective, Julie's surveillance ambitions had not lasted much past one in the morning. Not that I much felt the need to be watched. Even if somebody was out to get me, I doubted that anything would happen here at the house in Cohasset.

The air was cool and clean and smelled of salt and ozone. I popped back into the house to get my jacket and then headed down the back stairs to the beach. A walk along the shoreline has long been my personal prescription for wanderlust and insomnia. My bare feet, accustomed to New England beaches, ignored the discomfort of the surf-smoothed pebbles. Hopefully, a long walk would tire me enough to put me right off to sleep when I got back to the house.

The wash of the surf muffled all other sounds, so I had no warning of any other presence until the stones crunched nearby. I looked up, not surprised to see Krakow, the Dovers' Rhodesian Ridgeback, pattering down to the shoreline to join me. I rubbed his head affectionately, glad for his silent company, and walked on with my thoughts.

It was only about a half a mile to the breakwater, but that was usually enough to clear my head. The tide was out, on its way back in, as I climbed up on the rock hewn isthmus and carefully made my way along the ridge.

The Cohasset breakwater was not a noble edifice designed to protect sleeping ships from the furies of an angry sea. Oh no. This breakwater had a far more selfish objective. Its sole purpose was to hinder the migration of sediment from the north to the south, thereby creating a delightful beach on its northern side while robbing the sand from its southern neighbors. If the oldtimers were righteously angry about this larceny, it had never bothered me. If the shoreline in front of our house was rocky and bleak, having to walk the half mile to the public beach had never been that much of a hardship that it offset the benefit of having the company of the hordes of teenage hormones that would conjugate in that little sandy oasis.

Krakow barked once at my defection. He probably thought me a suicidal idiot, walking precariously along the crest of the breakwater.

Instead, he walked along the north side of the wall, some ten feet below me.

I walked out as far as I could. The tide was nearly out. On my left the beach was exposed but on my right, the shelf dropped off to a rocky, angry surf. I couldn't go all the way out to the end since the waves splashed up in dramatic spits, soaking anyone foolhardy enough to try it, but I went as far as I dared.

This was one of my favorite spots on the planet. As I sat, my feet dangling over the surf, looking off to the southeast, I could imagine myself shipwrecked on a solitary rock in the middle of the ocean, thousands of miles from civilization.

A loud crack from the public beach destroyed the illusion. It sounded like the lid of a dumpster being dropped. I looked over my shoulder, but it was an inky dark night and I could barely make out the silhouettes of the buildings that I knew were there, never mind any movement. Krakow started barking loudly.

"Shhhh!" I shushed him, to no avail. He continued to bark. As I rose to my feet, the dumpster crack echoed again, but this time something sharp struck the stones about five feet away from me. A small swirl of silt marked the point of contact.

I took half a step towards the trail of dust that still hung in the air. Another crack and I felt something buzz by my head. I brushed at it with my hand as if it were an insect. One last crack and two things hit me at the same moment: the realization that someone was shooting at me, and a numbing stab in my shoulder. The impact drove me back and I fell from the breakwater into the surf below.

CHAPTER TWENTY-FIVE

The room was white and smelt faintly of chlorine. I lay on a bed of crisp sheets. Muffled conversations, both near and far, were punctuated by the rhythmic pinging of monitoring equipment.

I turned my head and saw Tino, seated on a nearby chair, holding a remote control, looking up at a TV screen which was mounted near the ceiling. The Red Sox were playing an afternoon game.

I wanted to ask about the score but I needed to close my eyes for a second. When I opened them again, the window was dark and Julie sat in the chair, her eyes and fingers focused on her Gameboy. My eyes closed again.

I remembered falling into the water. I remembered a pain in my shoulder and then pain in my back and legs as I struck the rocks. But I couldn't remember how I had fallen into the water. Maybe I should ask Julie. I opened my eyes a crack.

Julie had turned back into Tino. This was getting confusing. Should I ask Tino how I fell into the water? When I opened my eyes again, Tino was gone and McBeige sat in the chair.

Oh knock it off, I thought irritably.

"Excuse me?" McBeige looked up from the

paper he had been reading.

I closed my eyes on purpose this time, hoping that when I opened them again, McBeige would be gone, but no such luck. He stood patiently over my bed, his obtrusive little tape recorder hovering near my head.

"I'm sorry to bother you, but I need to ask you a few questions."

I studied him for a moment. It was easier to think about what I saw in front of me than to try to figure out where I was and how I got there. The ubiquitous trench coat hung over the back of the chair. I wondered if he slept with it next to his bed.

"I need to ask you what happened Friday night." McBeige's voice was clinically impersonal.

"Last night? Or last Friday night?" My head swam and my voice sounded raspy.

"It's Monday afternoon. You're in the Weymouth General Hospital. You've been here all weekend."

It took me more than a minute to absorb this information. What happened to Saturday and Sunday? Since closing my eyes tended to make the situation more confusing, I opted for staring at the ceiling.

"I was walking on the breakwater and I fell off." I paused to think, bits and pieces slowly returned. "Krakow was barking."

I remembered hitting the water; striking the stones beneath. I couldn't make my arms work. No, it was just my right arm that wouldn't work. I looked down at it, willing it to move. It looked fine, but it just lay there. My left arm was laden with tubes and needles, but it responded properly. It was just my right arm that ignored me.

Memory came flooding back, unaccompanied by coherency.

"Dumpster!" I yelled.

I tried to sit up, but only managed to dislodge the I.V. tubes. A nurse hustled in and gave McBeige a hip-check to the boards as she came around to reattach the needle. She gave me a motherly smile before shooting a dagger glare at McBeige. McBeige squirmed appropriately. She'd have made a good nun.

"You okay now?" she asked. Her voice was a deep gravely bass. I looked at her more closely. I don't think she had been born a woman. Oh well, maybe not a nun then. She patted my wrist, threw another frown at McBeige, and left us alone.

"Somebody was shooting at me!"

McBeige didn't appear appropriately impressed by this.

"Bullets!" I clarified.

McBeige blinked.

"With a gun!" I still wasn't getting the response that I felt this news deserved.

Now let me explain something. I like guns. At least, I did until that Friday night. As a kid, my Dad would take me out to the range and teach me the rules and etiquette of guns. I like guns because there are rules about guns. Lots of rules about guns. And people who like guns like all those rules about guns. And the number one rule about guns is that you don't point them at other people.

And somebody was breaking that rule. Big time.

I calmed down to the point that I could (somewhat) coherently tell McBeige what I could remember of Friday night. I hadn't seen anyone. By the time I had figured out that someone was shooting at me, I was airborne and falling fast.

"Do you recall how many gunshots?"

I thought for a moment. "Four. I have no idea where the first one went. The second one hit a spot on the wall about five feet away to my left. The third was closer, a bit high and to my right. The fourth one hit my shoulder."

My instinct was to touch my right shoulder, to assure myself that it was alright, that despite getting shot I was still alive, but I stopped myself before I could dislodge the I.V. again. I didn't want Nurse Scratchit ticked at me.

"Do you recall from which direction the shots were fired?"

"From the public beach. At first I thought it was someone banging on the dumpster. It was too dark to see anything."

"And where was Scollari at this time?"

That question threw me for a loop. "Scollari? I don't know. Scollariworld?"

"He was first on the scene. He beat the Cohasset Police to the location. They were responding to reports of gunshots."

I stared at the dark TV screen overhead, wishing that it would suddenly pop on and explain to me what was happening.

"What does he say that he was doing there?" The old answer a question with a question ploy.

"He *says*," the emphasis on *says* did not lead me to believe that McBeige believed him, "He *says* that he was on surveillance, parked in the front of your house when he heard the shots. He claims to have run down the beach and found you floating face down in the water."

That was a very scary image. I decided to file that thought for later deliberation.

"Well, he and my sister were a lot more convinced of a threat to me than I was. They were taking turns keeping an eye on me. I really thought they were just being kind of lame, but in a cute sort of way, so when Julie fell asleep, I didn't think it would be that big of a deal to take a walk on the beach. It's possible that Tino had arrived sometime that night to relieve Julie and just camped outside."

"Or, it could be a handy alibi to cover up his presence at the scene of a crime."

I closed my eyes. McBeige took the hint and said goodbye. I didn't think him a bad person, but I really wondered if he was just too biased against Scollari to be effective on this case. If he was so convinced that it was Tino and he was wrong, he was going to be no help at all in finding the real shooter.

I knew that laying there in bed with all those painkillers that they had flowing through me probably didn't lead to the best conditions for deductive reasoning, but I didn't have much choice. I started to pick apart all the facts and look at them objectively.

My head hurt worse than my shoulder. I called for Nurse Scratchit to come give me more drugs.

CHAPTER TWENTY-SIX

"Phillip?" Julie shot at me.

I was too tired to respond with anything more than a derisive snort.

"Why not?"

I lay on the sofa in the sunroom, wondering how I could be so exhausted yet so restless at the same time. I kept one eye on Julie as she paced from one end of the room to the other. It was tiring to watch her, yet at the same time, I felt as if all my frustrations and fears and impatience were squirting out through her body.

"He may have had a motive to shoot Lucy, but I can't think of one reason why he would want to kill me. Between him and his mother, they've called about twenty times in the past week. He wants to get back together." I glanced over at all the montage of flowers, fruit baskets and candies that he had sent over in the past week.

"Do you?" Julie paused in her laps, looking at me closely.

I shot a glance over to where Tino sat motionlessly on one of the kitchen chairs, straddling it backwards, watching the two of us and saying nothing. I had no more intention of getting back with Phillip than I did of taking another moonlit walk on the beach, but I didn't feel comfortable discussing it in front of Tino. I contented myself with another eloquent snort and left it at that.

"How about Hogan O'Halloran? He seemed wicked pissed at you for screwing up the Salem Place foreclosure. I thought it was funny at the time, but forty dozen dead roses is pretty angry move."

I closed my eyes to think about it for a moment, but shook my head 'no' almost immediately. It didn't ring true to me.

"I don't think so. He's a player, like Dad was. His methods are different, but he's still playing the same game, and even if there was some payoff in killing me, it's just not worth the risk."

It was funny, but less than a week ago, I was pissing my pants because of O'Halloran's tactics, now they seemed silly and infantile. Nothing quite like a bullet to the shoulder to change your perspective on things.

"I think we should ask the police to check out O'Halloran's alibi, just to be on the safe side," said Tino quietly.

I looked over at Tino. He had said very little this evening, letting Julie ramble on with her questions and theories. Every time I had looked over at him, he appeared to be listening closely, but I could rarely read anything in his face. Now, however, I noticed a little skepticism in his eyes.

"Fine," I shrugged, closing my eyes for a moment. "I don't see the need in having the police question O'Halloran, but I can't see the harm in it either. There's just no motive there."

Then again, I couldn't see why anyone would want to kill me. I didn't think that I was an exceptionally wonderful person, but I also didn't think that I was so exceptionally bad that anyone would bother to shoot at me.

Apparently somebody disagreed.

A quiet comment from Tino made me open my eyes again.

"Sometimes a woman can make a man do things that he would never have done otherwise."

Julie and I glanced at Tino then stared at each other. Julie's eyes crinkled with laughter. Julie tended to find the strangest things amusing.

"And you speak from personal experience?" Julie's teasing made Tino smile, but it was a slightly twisted smile.

"It would surprise you."

A short interlude of silence followed this statement. Julie appeared to have exhausted her theories and I was just exhausted. It was left to Tino to restart the investigation.

"I don't want to pry, but I think it's important. Tell me about how the estate is set up."

I knew without opening my eyes that Julie was deferring this question to me. She had only the barest understanding of her inheritance. When Dad had died, I had administered the will. It was rather greedy of me. I don't mean that I grabbed all of the money, it was just that I had all the business and legal proceedings to go through to help distract me from my mourning. All Julie had was her grief.

"Other than the cash, the stock and some personal effects, all the assets were left in a series of trusts with both Julie and I as beneficiaries. While the trustees can use their discretion and dissolve them early, they're designed to be closed in the next five to ten years."

"Designed?" Tino asked.

The ache in my shoulder made me wince as I pushed myself up to a sitting position, but my enthusiasm for the subject made me ignore the pain.

"You see, Dad was an absolute genius when it came to real estate and tax laws. He's got each of these trusts set up to take advantage of a particular loophole in the tax code. We don't become liable for the bulk of the estate taxes until we liquidate the trusts. If the real estate values rise, then we use criteria A, if the market drops, then we use the alternate plan. There are a dozen different options given different economic conditions. The guy from the I.R.S. went over it with a fine tooth comb, but in the end he just laughed and said he had never seen anything so ingenious in his life. I think they're trying to pass some tax amendments to close up Dad's more inventive loopholes, but even if they do, if I stick to the plans, we will end up paying the least possible amount of taxes."

It was amazing how quickly I can turn two vibrant intelligent human beings into glassy-eyed zombies with such an efficient quantity of syllables.

"Let me ask this question another way," said Tino. "If anything happens to you, who gets the money?"

"Julie." I gave Tino the short answer.

"Free and clear?"

Boy, was I uncomfortable talking about this with him. I squirmed and looked over at Julie. No help there. She looked back at me like some fluffy bird, her head cocked to the side. I realized that she really didn't know how the estate was set up either.

"Depends. Currently, the trustees are myself, Julie and Uncle Bennie---"

"I'm a trustee?" Evidently, this was news to Julie.

"Yes, we discussed this before. Remember, you signed over a power of attorney so that I could handle the administration without having to bother you all the time."

"Oh, yeah." Julie's tone led me to believe that she didn't really remember that conversation. I wasn't surprised. These kinds of things just weren't that important to Julie.

"Most of the cash and stocks were used to pay off the initial estate taxes. The bulk of the estate is in income generating real estate. Uncle Benny handles the day to day operations. He only calls me in for big decisions, like when it's time to sell or buy a property."

"So if you were to die…?"

"I guess everything would go to Julie. I don't know, I'd have to ask Uncle Benny."

"So," Julie appeared to be having a revelation. "We don't have a lot of money in the bank?"

"Actually, no. We've got assets, and a healthy income from those assets, but until we start liquidating the trusts, we're only rich on paper."

"So could we have bailed out Tino if we had to?"

I don't know why I was so tempted to say no, but if the truth about the estate was important, I supposed I should be honest.

"It would have taken some maneuverings, we would either have had to liquidate some assets or borrow against collateral, but we could have done it."

I watched Julie closely. I could see I was giving her something to think about. If nothing else came out of this whole mess, maybe she would begin to realize that she couldn't keep going around promising to give people big chunks of money. Perhaps she was beginning to get the idea that there was a definite limit to our inheritance. I leaned back again and closed my eyes.

"Besides your Uncle Benny, what's the rest of your family like?"

"You're looking at it," said Julie.

"Hey! We've got those cousins in San Francisco!" I said. "And that Aunt in upstate New York!"

"Okay, two 'third cousins' in California that we've met twice---"

"Three times."

"I've met them twice; you've met them three times, and a great Aunt in upstate New York who may be dead for all we know."

"We get Christmas cards from her."

"Not since Dad died."

I bit my lip. Why did it bother me to admit in front of Tino that we had so little family?

"Tomorrow, if you're up to it, I'd like to visit your Uncle Benny," said Tino. "Couldn't hurt to ask him a few questions."

Julie and I exchanged glances.

Should we warn Tino about Uncle Benny? Julie asked me wordlessly.

No. I answered with my eyes. *There are some things that cannot be described, only experienced, and Uncle Benny is definitely on that list.*

CHAPTER TWENTY-SEVEN

The interior of Tino's Lincoln Towncar smelled like Tino: garlic and gunpowder, with the added aromas of motor oil and musty vinyl. The interior was silver and grey with an AM radio in the dashboard. An old undermounted CB radio was crowded by a police scanner and a vintage car phone. Not a cell phone, but one of those original bulky boxes with the cord that ran up to the handset. I picked it up, but wasn't surprised when I didn't get a dial tone.

The car was over twenty years old and it looked like Tino had been using it as a rolling office for nearly every day of it. A nearly empty pad of paper with a tethered pen was clipped to the visor. The carpet beneath the pedals was completely worn away showing two large ovals of metal undercarriage where his feet had rubbed it raw. The passenger seat, however, had very little wear and tear, and the back seat was as pristine as if it had just rolled off the show room.

I felt better this morning. Maybe not quite ready to run the marathon yet, but I thought I might make it through lunch without needing a nap.

Julie was in the back, her chin resting on the

back of the bench seat as she gave Tino directions to Uncle Benny's. I saw Tino's eyebrow lift when he was directed to take the Columbia Road off ramp, but he said nothing as he wove his way through the streets of Roxbury.

The fresh balmy warmth of spring had drawn the racks of wares from thrift stores out onto the sidewalks, which distracted your attention away from all the boarded up parochial schools that loomed behind them. These buildings, along with the once-elegant ten story brownstone apartment buildings and the dilapidated triple-deckers were relics of a more affluent era for Roxbury.

We made a slow progress down Columbus Ave, dodging adolescent pedestrians with delusions of indestructibility as they crisscrossed in front of the car. We finally turned off onto one of the less congested side streets.

The history of any village, big or small, can be told in its architecture, and Gleason Street was an eloquent little essay of the last two centuries of Roxbury. In the 1800s, little enclaves of semi-urban affluence sprung up in the form of Queen Anne row houses creating quaint little metropolitan neighborhoods. When the Anglo Americans moved on, the Irish Americans moved in. In the sixties, the area morphed into an African American community and, after surviving a period of decay and poverty, the homes now reflected the upwardly mobile lifestyles of the current residents.

Down the length of Gleason Street, there still

lived one elderly woman, a relict of the original Anglo residents, and two older Irish families, their children all grown and gone. The rest of the homes were owned by African American families and up and down the avenue the exteriors reflected the personal tastes and statuses of the residents. The facades ran the gamut from muted grays and whites to pastel palettes with their gingerbread trim picked out in rainbow hues. At Julie's direction, Tino parked in front of the most flamboyant of these painted ladies.

Uncle Benny's home-office was decorated in a tropical motif with desert pastels warring with Jamaican primaries. Eight towering potted palm trees bordered the walkway, having spent the frigid New England winter in the two story greenhouse hidden behind the house. Plastic flamingoes and rock gardens filled with seashells only added to the aura of a Caribbean cabana.

I don't know why, but every time I stepped on the walkway that led up to Uncle Benny's house, the air felt about five degrees warmer.

With my right arm still pretty useless, my left hand struggled with the car door. Tino circled the car and opened both mine and Julie's doors simultaneously, but his eyes scanned the neighborhood. I thought I could detect a certain amount of curiosity in his normally stoic expression, so perhaps a note of clarification might be in order.

"Um, Uncle Benny is not, technically, a biological relative."

Julie's giggle preceded Uncle Benny's entrance by mere seconds. The door flung open and in moments I was enveloped in a coconut oil tsunami.

"No! No! No! My little copper angel! I know I did not tell you not to get shot at, but now I do! Do not get shot at! Do you hear me! Do not do such a thing again!"

It was pointless to explain to Uncle Benny that getting shot was not an elective.

I gave a little yelp as his hugging jostled my shoulder and he immediately leapt back as if burnt by a flame.

"And why are you outside in this icy cold when you are so hurt? Come in! Come in! Come in!"

For Uncle Benny, a mild day in May was arctic. Only in the depths of a July heat wave could he be heard to enjoy New England weather. Herding us into the house, he stopped to wave cheerfully at one of his neighbors.

"Bonjou, Madam Coblyn! Miserable day, is it not?"

Mrs. Coblyn sat in a rocking chair on her front porch, obviously torn between disapproval of her bizarre neighbor and glee that he had once again provided her with some delightful gossip fodder. She watched us closely while she dialed the small phone that she kept on her lap.

No one who lives in New England, not even a full-blooded Haitian like Uncle Benny, can naturally have skin as dark as his. Since he wasn't able to vacation in the Caribbean more than twice a year, I strongly suspected he maintained his dark mahogany hue with a sunlamp. He always smelled of coconut butter and exotic Haitian spices. He was short, a little less than my five foot four inch height, and as thin as a high tension power line. He crackled with so much energy that his long coarse dreadlocks danced on his scalp like the snakes of Medusa.

A wall of heat hit us as we entered the front door. The thermostat had to be set at eight-five, which was slightly irrational since huge palm frond ceiling fans spun futilely trying to find some cool air to circulate.

Uncle Benny led us into the front parlor which was decorated with white wicker furniture with Caribbean accessories. The textured wallpaper looked like grass skirting and drapes of beaded bamboo hung in the windows. He even had little sand dunes dotted with seashells lining the sills. It always reminded me of the Howell's hut on Gilligan's Island.

"Nice suit," I commented as he poured out four tall glasses of pink fruit juice. When he first came out of the house, I had been relieved to see him wearing a very well cut suit of dark blue serge. Of course, the bright Hawaiian print shirt with an eight inch wide fuchsia floral tie and the turquoise plastic flip flop sandals weren't precisely classic Wall Street, but it was a lot better than the paisley loincloth he had been known to be wearing when he answered the door.

"Julie called me earlier and told me you were coming," said Uncle Benny. "Someone important to meet, so I dress for the occasion."

He turned to hand Tino a glass of juice. "Are you the important someone I am to meet?"

"Uncle Benny, this is Tino Scollari." Julie was beaming. "He's my boss. We're private detectives and we're working on solving the murder of Lucy Rudd!"

Tino glanced at me and shook his head ruefully. Julie made it sound like they were playing Malibu Barbie.

"Lucy Rudd! Loopy crud! I do not care about this Loosy dud!" Uncle Benny shook his finger into Julie's face. "Who is shooting at your sister? That is a bigger question, no?"

"That's why we're here." As Tino spoke, Uncle Benny whipped around to aim his loaded digit at his new target. "We think the murder of Lucy Rudd is connected with Jo's attacker. We want to ask you some questions."

An uncomfortable silence settled on the room as Uncle Benny locked eyes with Tino.

"You think that whoever shot this Lulu Mudd was trying to kill our little Jo? And you think I am suspect?"

"No! Of course not!" Julie answered quickly.

"Well you should!" Uncle Benny spun his finger back into Julie's face. "Everyone is suspect! Everyone is guilty until proven innocent!"

He lowered his finger as he turned to glare at

Tino. "You ask! I shall tell!" He plumped down on the sofa, folded his arms and waited for Tino's questions.

In the face of such an invitation, Tino was a little speechless. Uncle Benny clapped his hands impatiently.

"Speak! Ask! What do you wish to know?"

I don't think Tino was used to having this little control over a situation and I bit back a grin as I watched him struggle with the reins.

"Julie mentioned that you weren't a biological uncle. Could you explain how you came to be their trustee?"

Oh good. I leaned back in my chair and prepared to enjoy the moment. Uncle Benny was a great story teller, and this was one my favorite Cinderella stories.

"Many years ago, before even the little copper angel was born, I came to this country from Haiti. After many, many months of effort, I became a cab driver. I worked very hard at being a cab driver and soon I was the very worst cab driver in all of Boston. I got eight tickets and wrecked three cars in less than one year. I was a very bad cab driver. They take away my license, yet still I drive my cab. They put me in jail for six months, the food was not bad, and when I get out, still I drive my cab. I was, without doubt, the worst cab driver in Boston.

"One day, my cousin André is home sick, so I borrow his medallion and go to the airport. There, I pick up Joe D'Angelo. He was coming back from

New York and he needs a ride to the Back Bay. I say 'Sure, Mista!' and off we go.

"The traffic was very bad. Your dad and I be laughing and talking. Ah, but he was a funny man. I get off on the wrong ramp and soon we are lost in East Boston. I say, 'Don't you worry, I know a short cut!' But East Boston is very tricky and I cannot find the street to get out. So I tell Mista Joe 'I want to show you something,' so he does not know how very lost I am.

"I take him by the abandoned warehouses down on E-street and I say 'look at these old buildings! I have a cousin that works for a trucking company and they go from their depot in Chelsea to the docks in Charlestown to the customs terminal at the airport ten times a day! Someone should buy these old buildings and fix them up and then rent them to the trucking companies. Someone does that before they start fixing the Chelsea Street bridge and everyone else figures out that it is faster to go here than Chelsea!'

"And Mista Joe, he says, 'Stop the car!' So I do and he gets out and stares at the buildings. Then he says to me, 'Do you know any other buildings like this?' And I say, 'Sure, Mista Joe!' so we spend the whole day driving around Boston and I show him all the buildings that I think someone should buy and fix up because they could be worth big bucks.

"When I finally drop him off in Back Bay, the meter says two hundred ninety two dollars and eight five cents. He gives me three hundred dollars and says, 'Keep the change!'

"I say 'thanks a lot big spender!' and he laughs and gives me his card and says to me: 'Benny, you are one helluva lousy cab driver, but you have got an eye for real estate. I'd like you to come and work for me. Come by my office tomorrow.'

"'What? Do you want me to drive for you?' I ask.

"'No, Benny,' He says. 'I will never let you drive me again. You are one helluva lousy driver.'

"'What are you talking about Mista Joe? Did I hit one pedestrian all day? I think I did pretty good!'"

Uncle Benny leaned back in his chair with a deep chuckle. His dreadlocks bounced as he shook his head as if to jar loose a few more memories.

"That was almost thirty years ago. First I just work in the office, then I save my paychecks and Joe let's me invest in one of his projects and soon I have built a big portfolio all of my own. I own buildings and houses here and in Haiti, and a warehouse in South Carolina and two strip malls in Toronto. I have so much money, I have sponsored eleven of my cousins to come to this country, and now they work for me helping me run my buildings."

Uncle Benny smiled at me. "Your father trusted me with his business and he trusted me with his daughters." He turned to face Tino. "I have known these girls since they were noisy little babies and I do not want people shooting at them. You tell me what you are doing to stop bad people from shooting at my girls."

Uncle Benny met Tino's gaze unblinkingly. As usual, Tino's face told me little about what he was thinking. Above his jaw, a muscle gave the slightest twitch but I couldn't tell if it was amusement or anger. His eyes and voice were emotionless.

"We're trying to explore all possible motives, and it would be helpful if you could tell us exactly how the trust is set up."

A moment passed before Uncle Benny slowly nodded. "It is not one trust, eighteen different trusts. Each of them has ownership of a particular asset. Some trusts own the property in full, some have a controlling interest, some have a minority interest. Regardless, all the trusts were set up the same way. The original trustees were Joe D'Angelo, Little Jo and myself with the original beneficiaries being Mista Joe and the girls. When Mista Joe died, the remaining two trustees, Jo and I elected Julie to be the third trustee. The girls are the only beneficiaries now."

"And if something happened to either Jo or Julie...?"

"The remaining sister would be the only beneficiary and she and I would have to elect a third trustee to administer the trust."

"And who would be the most likely candidate for that third trustee, should that happen?" There was a restrained intensity in Tino's question.

I looked at Uncle Benny. Uncle Benny looked at me. We both looked at Julie. Julie looked behind her, over her shoulder. Then she looked back at us. We all shrugged.

"I do not really want to have that discussion," Uncle Benny said softly, his eyes on me. "But I think perhaps we should think about it."

I racked my head for suggestions. I opened and closed my mouth several times, but bit back my words before they even got halfway out. My first choices, Phillip or one of his parents, were now out of the question. Julie was right about the cousins in California and the aunt in upstate New York; we barely knew them.

"How about Sister Benignus?" I blurted out in desperation.

That suggestion was met with the silence it deserved. |

"How about Ant Bee?" offered Julie.

"*Bondye!* No! No! No! I would rather have the cranky nun!" Uncle Benny's arms waved in the air in a plea to heaven.

"Maybe we should work on keeping Jo alive rather than lining up her replacement," said Tino quietly.

"I like that idea better." I grabbed at the opportunity to turn the subject.

We stayed for another half hour with nothing much more of the case being discussed. Julie and Uncle Benny laughed and chatted. Once or twice I heard Tino's chuckle, but I was too tired to join in. Perhaps my prediction that I could make it through lunch without a nap was a bit overly optimistic. My shoulder started throbbing again and I slipped one of the pills that I had been given. I slouched down on the sofa and closed my eyes for a moment.

"I think maybe we should get Joey home before she starts drooling on Uncle Benny's furniture." I heard Tino say. Julie chuckled in response.

I roused myself to glare at Tino. "It's 'Jo', not 'Joey'." I pushed myself back up to a sitting position and Tino grabbed my left elbow to help me to my feet. I swayed dizzily for a moment, bumping against his chest, secretly grateful for the buttress.

As Uncle Benny showed us to the door, he handed a fat envelope to Julie.

"Jo, I'm giving the Raleigh Street papers to Julie. You take a look at them when you are feeling better."

I snorted in response. I knew what those documents would say.

"Don't you snort at me, young lady!" Uncle Benny was now shaking his finger into my face. "You just read those papers and we will talk about them later."

I snorted again. Not very lady-like, but very expressive. Uncle Benny grabbed my face with his hands and kissed both my cheeks and then my forehead before giving my head a little shake of frustration.

"You are stubborn, like your father! But much prettier!"

I smiled and gave Uncle Benny a kiss back on his cheek. "I'll read them tonight. I promise."

Minutes later, I was re-ensconced in the front seat of Tino's Towncar. I rested my head against the cool glass for a moment before settling back onto the seat. Tino grabbed the seat belt shoulder strap and slipped it behind my back. I slumped gratefully onto the benchseat and pillowed my head on my left arm. Bucket seats are vastly over-rated.

In the backseat, I could hear Julie thumbing through the file.

"So, what's this all about?" she asked.

"Uncle Benny's got a hot offer on the Raleigh Street property, but the trust isn't scheduled to be liquidated for another three years."

"What are you going to do?"

"Wait the three years, like Daddy said."

There was a long pause and more rattling of papers before Julie spoke again. "I don't know, Jo. I think what Uncle Benny is saying is that this offer is so high, we would get a lot more money, even after taxes, if we sold now."

"Maybe. But Daddy said."

CHAPTER TWENTY-EIGHT

The late afternoon sun piercing through a crack in the drapes was not as disturbing to my sleep as Ant Bee muttering up and down the stairs.

I don't remember the ride back from Uncle Benny's. I'm pretty sure I was fast asleep long before we hit Route 93. I woke briefly when we got back to Cohasset and Tino carried me up the stairs, but quickly fell back to sleep when I hit the bed. I hadn't slept well. The painkillers had worn off and my shoulder woke me with a deep ache.

I felt very sulky and very sorry for myself. On T.V. they make a big deal about it when someone gets shot, but they never talk about how *long* it hurts. I was glad that I was alone at the moment because I was much too grouchy for company.

I shook off my funk and headed to the bathroom.

Another thing they never mention on T.V. is how hard it is to shower with your shoulder all bandaged and your right arm hanging lamely.

I sat in the tub with the handheld shower nozzle and rinsed the shampoo from my hair. I soaped myself down, and then gingerly shaved my legs with my left hand, taking care not to nick my shins.

I lay back and rinsed off the soap, carefully avoiding the bandages on my shoulder. The water felt warm and soft as it ran down my legs.

"Here we go, Joey," he had said as lifted me out of the car. He does that just to annoy me, call me Joey. I could tell by that note in his voice, he was just looking for a reaction. I would have said something, but I was too groggy. I would have hit him, but my left arm was pinned against his chest and my right arm was pretty useless. So I went to bite him. But as I buried my face into his shirt, I was distracted by the scent of his chest. Garlic and gunpowder and something else. Something musky smelling, something very male smelling. My eyes closed as I tried to recall and identify that elusive scent.

I dropped the shower nozzle with a clatter when I realized what I was doing. Oh, my God! Here I am in the tub, playing with the shower massage, and thinking about my sister's boyfriend.

No amount of rosaries could save me this time. I was definitely going to burn in hell.

I jarred my arm in my haste to get out of the tub. I gasped as the stabbing pain in my shoulder made my vision go all white for a second. *See?* I could almost hear Sister Benignus' voice saying. *This is what happens to girls who play with the massage nozzle in the shower!*

I pulled on a pair of sweat pants and a sleeveless terry sweatshirt that zipped up the front and clashed horribly. I didn't bother with a bra and I had no makeup on. I fingered combed my hair, it would be frizzy and horrible within twenty minutes. I took a quick look in the mirror and sighed. I couldn't even get into a grunge club looking like this. Oh well, I'd just be downstairs with Ant Bee for the night. She'd lived through communism. She'd seen worse.

The house was quiet as I came down the stairs. The grandfather clock ticked at me. Four thirty. I had slept through lunch and I was starved.

"Ant Bee?" I called as I came around the corner. "Is there anything left over from..."

I froze as I became aware of Tino and Julie in the sunroom. Julie was sitting on the sofa, her feet curled under her. She had been staring at Tino, but turned to smile at me. Tino was standing by the table, reading what appeared to be the Raleigh Street Proposal. For a moment as he looked up, I caught a flash of something that looked like disappointment flicker over his face, but then the stony mask slipped into place.

But it was enough. I knew that he was completed disgusted with my appearance. My first flare of guilt and embarrassment over the shower head incident was completely eclipsed by a blazing resentment over his attitude.

That my anger was totally irrational and out of proportion to his actions is completely irrelevant.

I marched into the room, my hand extended to snatch the papers from him.

"Those are private." I snapped.

Completely unfazed by my behavior, Tino lifted the papers above his head, out of my reach.

"And I am investigating. Hence the title 'Private Investigator'. Rule seventeen of Private Investigation: don't be polite and wait for permission." He smiled down at me. "You should take notes, this is important training."

I stopped my futile and slightly embarrassing attempt to grab the papers and glared at him. "Since I have no intention of *ever* being a private investigator," I spat the words at him, "I'll spare the effort."

"Pity," he said. "You have good instincts."

My anger flared as I recalled where I'd heard him say something similar before. "You need to get some new pick up lines. You're repeating yourself."

That managed to wipe the smile off of Tino's face. A vein pulsed in his cheek as he clenched his jaw. His eyes narrowed and he looked as if he was going to say something, but opted instead for a cold glare. A frigid silence ensued.

Julie jumped in to fill the void. "I told Tino he could look at the file, Jo. We've got to examine every angle in an investigation."

I waited a few more seconds, holding Tino's gaze before breaking off to answer Julie.

"Sounds like *someone* has been taking notes."

I would like to say that I then walked gracefully over to the sofa and sat myself down with poise and authority.

Instead I bumped into the coffee table, stubbed

my toe on the leg, lost my balance and fell shoulder first onto the couch. I bit back a whimper, but rolled over quickly in a vain attempt to make it look like I meant to do that.

Tino tapped the file folder rhythmically on the back of the chair, torn between bewilderment at my attitude and amusement at my clumsiness. After a moment, he turned his attention back to the file in his hand.

"This is quite the deal that Uncle Benny has lined up," he said as he paged through the documents. "It's a twenty million dollar offer on that property. He seems to think that the price is twice the fair market value and that you won't see another offer this high for another ten or twenty years."

I shrugged. It was no more than Uncle Benny had repeated to me four or five times already.

Tino looked back down at the notes. "Why is it that the trust will only get twelve million dollars? What happens to the other eight million?"

"Uncle Benny has a 40% interest in that property. The trust has a 60% interest."

"So you're holding up the sale could, in essence, be costing Uncle Benny about four million dollars."

I shrugged again. "If your thinking that Uncle Benny would kill me in order to liquidate the trust, all I can say is that you don't know Uncle Benny."

"All I'm saying is that four million dollars should not be ignored as a possible motive for murder," said Tino gently.

A grunt of skepticism escaped my throat. "Even if he were desperate for the money, he'd try to talk Julie into voting with him before he tried to, um, eliminate me."

I glanced over a Julie. Her brow was furrowed with an unpleasant thought.

"What?" I asked.

"Well," Julie's voice wavered. "Uncle Benny has spoken to me a couple of times about this. I just told him that you took care of that kind of stuff and that I trusted you to handle it."

The room was quiet as I tried to force my brain into accepting the possibility that Uncle Benny could possibly try to hurt me. I stood up suddenly and walked to French doors, pushing back the sheers to look out at the surf.

I tried to visualize Uncle Benny, standing in an alley in Dorchester, waiting to shoot six bullets at a woman he thought was me. I tried to imagine him hiding in the dark at the public beach, taking pot shots into the night. I shook my head. I simply couldn't connect the two images.

"The thing is," my voice was just barely loud enough for me to hear, "Uncle Benny is the only person left that knew me as a baby."

The idea that one of the last "grown-ups" left in my life could possibly be trying to kill me was overwhelming. I shook my head again, more violently this time and turned to face Tino and Julie. When I spoke, my voice was clipped and matter of fact. If I couldn't deal with the possibility that Uncle

Benny was the killer, than I'd better figure out who it was. And quickly.

"What was the caliber of the gun that shot at me on the beach?"

The sudden strength in my voice made Julie and Tino straighten alertly. It was Tino who answered.

"The police weren't able to recover any of the bullets. The tide was coming in and the search area was too widespread."

"How about the one from my shoulder?"

"It glanced off the bone and passed through. They weren't able to recover that one either."

"And the gun that killed Lucy was a .38, probably a revolver."

Tino eyed me intently. "How did you know it was a .38?"

I stopped my pacing, halted as much by the note of suspicion in his voice as by my own confusion. How did I know it was a .38?

"I heard you and Detective McBeige talking about it at the police station." I said after a moment's recollection.

"McBeige?"

Oops. "I mean, McAdams."

Tino chuckled at the nickname, but I thought I saw a sliver of doubt in his eyes.

"What makes you think it was a revolver?"

I shrugged. "Six shots. Seems to me that someone emptied the cylinder. Could have been an automatic or a semi, but then why stop at six?"

Tino nodded reluctantly.

"The shooter is probably fairly experienced, too." I went on. "Hitting Lucy six out of six times from a medium range takes either some skill or a lot of luck. But, being able to hit me, in the dark, on a moonless night, from more than a hundred feet away, I'm guessing our killer knows his way around a gun."

"Or 'her way'," said Julie.

We both turned to look at Julie.

"You keep saying 'he', but it could be a 'she'. *Must explore all angles.*"

I restrained the impulse to roll my eyes. The only female suspects were Julie and I.

"Julie's right," said Tino. "Never exclude any possibility until it's been eliminated by the evidence."

My pacing had brought me behind Tino's back, so I took that opportunity to stick my tongue out at him. Julie bit back a laugh.

"I saw that." Tino lied.

I stopped my pacing to stare at the door to Dad's study. I must have been too quiet for too long, because Tino turned to stare at me, an eyebrow raised in question.

"Fine," I said after a moment. "Let's eliminate."

I turned and ran back up the stairs to my bedroom. I grabbed my purse, resolutely ignoring the mirror as I passed it, and hurried back down. Tino and Julie were still there, staring at the spot where I had exited. I walked between them and over to the door to Dad's study, the two of them followed in my wake.

Behind Dad's desk stood a tall, heavy, mahogany credenza. Its two solid doors were ornately carved with the images of stags leaping through leafy forests. I rooted around the bottom of my purse and pulled out a small ring of keys. I segregated one the keys and placed it into the small lock that was cleverly concealed within the unblemished woodwork. Tino, coming up behind me, grabbed my wrist as I started to open the doors.

"Watch for fingerprints," he warned.

"Too late for the outside," I said. "Ant Bee polishes the woodwork in here on Tuesdays and Fridays."

The doors swung open to reveal my father's collection. I hadn't touched his rifles since his death and I could tell that they hadn't been disturbed in years. Despite Ant Bee's fanatical diligence, a faint layer of dust could be seen coating them. The security cable still draped between their trigger casings and the padlock hung as a mute sentry.

Using one of the keys as a hook, I pulled out the lower drawer to display the period pistols. Much less dust had penetrated here and all of the slots were filled, present and accounted for. The center slot was draped with dark blue velvet. I pulled back the cloth to reveal the pride of Dad's collection, an 1822 Flintlock. The security cables were all intact, the trigger locks all in place.

Checking out the bottom drawer was just

routine. None of those handguns were .38 caliber. I slid the drawer shut again, using the key as a lever, and pulled open the drawer above it.

Eight handguns were neatly nestled into eight slots. All eight guns were secured with trigger locks and the padlocked security cable threaded laconically through the casings. I could tell by looking at them that they hadn't been disturbed for months, but I unlocked the cable to double check.

Using a pen from Dad's desk, I lifted my Undercover .38 revolver. I sniffed it quickly, checked to be sure that it had been cleaned as thoroughly as I always left my guns, and placed it back into its slot. The Undercover was my first gun. Dad bought it for me when I was fourteen. But it was a five shot, so even if someone had gotten this far in to the gun cabinet, I doubted that this would have been the weapon. I checked Dad's .38 semi and came up the same. Then I lifted the .38 Smith and Wesson. The six shot. If the killer was someone close enough to me to get in to the gun cabinet, this is the one that would have been the most likely candidate.

I set the gun down on Dad's desk and unlocked the trigger lock. Using a letter opener and a pen, I opened the cylinder and peered inside.

I shook my head.

"No?" asked Julie.

"No." I answered.

"You sure?" asked Tino.

I nodded. "Nobody cleans guns like I do. Dad

used to say that I was the most meticulous gun cleaner he'd ever met."

"I think the term he used was 'anal retentive'," offered Julie unhelpfully.

I turned and gave her the baleful stare which that comment deserved.

"When was the last time you had these guns out?" asked Tino.

I shrugged. "Not since Dad died."

Julie's eyebrows showed her surprise.

"Phillip doesn't shoot and it's no fun going to the range by yourself." I answered her unasked question.

I re-mounted the trigger lock and returned the gun to its slot. I checked the ammo drawer to be on the safe side as well. To say the truth, I don't remember how many boxes we had in there, it had been a couple of years, but it looked undisturbed. I closed and relocked the cabinet.

"Well, that doesn't *prove* anything. It doesn't really *eliminate* anyone either, but I think I can say with confidence that it wasn't one of my own guns that shot at me."

"If it's okay with you, I'd like to ask McAdams to have the case fingerprinted, inside and out, just to be sure, and to have all three .38's tested for ballistic matches to the Rudd bullets."

"Sure. I'm surprised they didn't do it when I was under arrest."

Tino gave his half smile. "They were planning to, but when Julie showed up with her evidence, the judge denied the search warrant. I know that McAdams was going to ask you to voluntarily allow it, but you got shot before he could ask."

I must have looked perplexed because Tino felt compelled to add, "He called me yesterday about it."

"Hmmph. I wonder why he didn't ask me when he was here."

"When was he here?"

"The day I was arrested. He showed up here late that afternoon to, um…"

"Warn you about me?"

I met his eyes, uncertain as to how to respond to this. Julie bit her lip as she looked from Tino to me. A long couple of seconds passed. My stomach rumbled with hunger, which made Tino smirk. My eyes narrowed, but before I could respond, the phone on the desk began to ring. I glanced over at the caller I.D. A number I didn't recognize with a Boston exchange. I could hear Ant Bee pick up the phone in the kitchen. After a moment, I heard her walk into the sunroom.

"Call for ju, *Ms.* D'Angelo," she announced, her voice deceptively monotone.

Through the doorframe I could see her standing in the middle of the sunroom, a sandwich on a plate in one hand, the portable phone in the other.

I went back to my face off with Tino. "Who is it?"

She gave me the Hungarian pffft, which, in this circumstance, I interpreted as meaning "What? Am

I your secretary?"

I sighed, broke off glaring at Tino and went back into the sunroom to pick up the phone.

"Thanks," I mumbled halfheartedly to Ant Bee, referring to both the phone and the peanut butter sandwich. I rather foolishly took a large bite before I picked up the receiver. "Hawo?"

"D'Angelo?" The voice on the phone was male and vaguely familiar, but I couldn't place it yet.

"Yeb." I swallowed dryly and looked around for something to wet my mouth with. Nothing out here. I headed for the kitchen.

"We need to talk."

And what are we doing now?

"Okay." I said as I rooted around in the back of the fridge, looking for a bottle of water that didn't look like it was recycled tap water. No luck. I grabbed a bottle with a broken seal, wedged it between my knees so that I could open it with my left hand, and chugged.

"Tomorrow. Ten A.M. My office."

I still couldn't place the voice. "Excuse me, who am I speaking with?"

I quickly retreated from the kitchen, evicted by Ant Bee's territorial glare. Julie and Tino had returned to the sunroom and Julie gave me the "who is it?" look. I shrugged and rolled my eyes.

"I had a visitor this morning," said the voice.

This guy was starting to bug me.

"I'm very happy for you. Who is this?"

"Don't fuck with me, D'Angelo."

The phone clicked dead in my hand. I stared at the receiver in disbelief. "O'Halloran?"

"O'Halloran?" Julie echoed my amazement.

"I think so. He didn't say who it was, but I think it was him. He's such a unique conversationalist."

Tino turned and strode back into the study. I picked up the sandwich and followed.

"What did he want?" Julie asked, following me into the study.

Tino was at the desk, jotting down the number from the caller I.D. He opened my laptop and started tapping away.

"Please," I said sarcastically, "help yourself."

"Do we need to review rule seventeen so soon?" Tino looked up from the keyboard just enough so that I could catch that annoying grin. "You really should have some security on this thing. Your basic password will stop most hackers."

"Usually common courtesy is enough security for most of my houseguests."

"Really? Maybe it's time you expanded your circle of friends a little."

I circled around behind him to peek at what he was up to.

"Omigod! You're a two finger typer!"

I had never seen a two finger typer move so fast. I'm guessing he was clocking about fifty to sixty words per minute.

"My fingers are too big to type any other way," he said, his eyes scanning the screens as they flashed by.

I checked out his hands. He did have very large fingers. I recall someone telling me something about men with large hands. I think it was in college. I think it was good. I think it was...

I wave of heat hit my face as I remembered what it was.

Tino, perhaps sensing this, looked up and gave me a very disturbing smile. "There are other things that I do that I use all ten fingers for."

I had no response for that. I shoved the sandwich into my mouth.

"Mmmm?" I said. It could have meant anything. I just hope he couldn't finger out, I mean, figure out, what I was thinking.

He turned back to read the screen. "Yes, the call came from O'Halloran's office."

"So, what did he want?" Julie asked again.

"He wants to meet me at his office tomorrow morning."

"Why?" asked Julie.

"He didn't say."

"So are you going?" she asked.

"Are you kidding?" I licked some peanut butter off my wrist where it had dripped. "Someone out there is trying to kill me. I'm hiding under my bed."

Tino was leaning against the desk, thinking. "I'll call McAdams. We'll get the police to back us up. Wire you up with a transmitter and a G.P.S.---"

My jaw hung open. I'm sure that Tino had a brilliant view of the half chewed sandwich in my mouth. "What part of 'no' is not penetrating?"

"A Kevlar vest?" Julie offered.

Tino nodded.

"A what?" I felt like I was being stampeded from both sides.

"Kevlar," Tino explained, "a bullet-proof vest."

"But try not to get shot. It hurts like hell," Julie said with a bright smile. "It feels like someone kicking you in the chest."

I was having trouble breathing again. I don't know which was more scary, the idea that someone might try to shoot me again, or that Julie evidently had firsthand experience with getting shot while wearing a bullet proof vest. I turned a glassy stare towards her.

"Tokyo," she added, as if that explained all.

"Oh," I said faintly.

CHAPTER TWENTY-NINE

"It's no use." I fell backwards onto the bed, spilling the pile of suits onto the floor.

Julie nodded. It was pointless to argue.

"What's the matter?" Tino's voice echoed from the landing outside the bedroom door.

"Kevlar is not slimming," I yelled.

There was an eloquent silence coming from the other side of the door. Julie looked at me, biting her lip in silent laughter. Despite the current wardrobe crisis and the lurking roil of dread in my stomach, I couldn't help but grin back.

"Sorry Jo," said Julie as she reached for one of the suits that had fallen behind the bed, "we have no choice."

"No, please!" I begged. "Anything but that!"

"It's the only one that will button over the vest, everything else is too tight."

I covered my head with a pillow to block out the gruesome vision of Julie standing there holding the pink and green plaid thrift store horror that I had bought to rag on Lucy.

God was getting back at me.

I wondered if I could fake everyone out by making them think that I died. Maybe if I lay real still, they'd all think that I accidentally suffocated myself with the pillow and then they'd go away.

"C'mon Jo." Julie slapped at my foot. "Let's get going."

I sighed and pulled the pillow off my head. Maybe if I put extra mascara on, no one will notice the suit.

❦

"What's wrong with your eyes?" asked Tino.

Okay, so maybe I went a little too heavy on the eyeliner, but at least no one commented on the suit. Yet.

I had reached an entirely new depth of discomfort. The Kevlar vest was heavy and pressed painfully against the wound in my shoulder. The little G.P.S. tracking bug was wedged under my bra and dug into my boob. The listening bug was duct taped to my belly and scratched like hell. Tino wouldn't let me take my pain pills because he said that I needed to be fully alert. And the only shoes that would possibly go with this outfit pinched my toes horribly.

I was a tad grouchy.

I was to be dropped off in a taxi. McBeige was playing cab driver. It was a car that the police department kept for undercover operations. It looked very genuine. I peeked through the plexi-divider and checked out the front seat.

"Where's the trenchcoat?" I asked McBeige.

He shot me a look before answering. "In the trunk."

"Oh good." I settled back into my seat. "I was worried."

From where the cab stopped, I could see the white plumber's van parked on the other side of New Chardon Street. Tino, Julie and the police technicians would be waiting in there. I resisted the urge to wave.

I reached through the little window and handed McBeige a dollar.

"Keep the change."

He worked at keeping a smile off his face. Not too successful.

"Try not to get shot at," he said as I left the cab.

I leaned back in. "I'm wearing a pink and green plaid suit. Getting shot would be redundant."

I turned and looked up at the O'Halloran building and shuddered. Sixteen stories of concrete were just barely relieved by narrow boring windows set in an uninspired array. Bulky, intimidating and unimaginative, it made the South Bay House of Corrections look inviting. I whooshed out a deep breath, straightened my shoulders and walked inside.

There was no lobby, only a narrow hall that led to a shallow foyer. I walked past closed office doors and checked out the directory that was posted between the elevators.

"O'Halloran's office is on the sixteenth floor," I muttered for the benefit of my listening audience. I stepped into a waiting elevator.

Up until that morning, I hadn't disliked the color mint green, but after walking into O'Halloran's office, I was never able to stomach it again. You wouldn't think that there were so many different shades of mint green, and that they would all clash so badly when crammed together. Carpets, walls, cubicle dividers, desks, were all different hues of that pale jade. Apparently O'Halloran enforced some sort of dress code on his minions because all of the office staff appeared to be wearing similar shades. I felt like I was underwater in some algae filled pool.

A tall thin wraith of green detached itself from the maze of cubicles and approached me. His movements were so willowy that I glanced down to see if he had little wheels on the bottom of his shoes or if he was floating off the ground. He stopped a couple of feet away from me and struck a pose.

"Can I help you?" were his words, but his attitude was anything but helpful.

"I'm here to see Hogan O'Halloran. I have an appointment."

He looked me up and down, taking a couple of extra seconds to absorb the glory of my outfit. "And you would be?" He asked with a sniff.

"Jo D'Angelo." I decided to go with the 'and-why-aren't-you-wearing-pink-and-green-plaid' attitude.

He tossed his head back and spun on his heel, gliding back through the office. I followed him down an aisle made of mint green cubicles where mint green drones kept their eyes focused onto their mint green desktops. There was very little conversation breaking up the tap tap of computer keyboards. No chatter. No laughter. It was if I'd stumbled onto one of the outer rings of hell.

The corridor ended at a lone elevator door. Elf-boy pressed the button and the doors immediately glided open.

"A private elevator?" I commented.

Elf-boy ignored me and stepped into the small chrome chamber. I followed, and in the convention of all elevators riders, turned and stood beside him, staring at the door. There were only five buttons on the control panel. *16, 1, A, B* and *C.* He waved a small wand over the control panel and then pressed "*C*". The doors closed silently and we descended. I didn't have a good feeling about this and I stole a glance over to check out Elf-boy. He appeared to be struggling with some inner conflict. The doors opened and he held them back with his arm as I stepped out.

"Nice suit," he muttered as if the words were wrenched out of him despite his best efforts. With a sniff and a toss of his head he stepped to the back of the elevator and eyed my skirt with a sort of petulant envy as the door closed between us.

I was alone, but I could hear some arrhythmic thumping nearby. As I slowly headed towards the sounds, I scoped out this part of the building. The concrete walls were painted grey and fluorescent lights added to the antiseptic feel. I walked pass a darkened, glass-walled room filled with state of the art exercise equipment. No people though. It had this vacant, unused feel to it as if no one in the building had access to this area. From up ahead, I could see light pouring from another glass walled room. It was from here that the thumping came from. As I walked towards the sounds, I whispered softly so that they could hear me out in the van.

"I'm on sub-level C. It looks like an unused health facility but someone is down here. I can hear them up ahead."

Slowly, I approached the lit room.

"Squash!" I muttered. I stood in the shadow for a moment and watched as O'Halloran chased an innocent little ball around a glass cage and then smacked it with his racket.

Evidently, the mint green dress code did not extend to Mr. O'Halloran. He was dressed in a white crew top with white shorts. A towel was draped artistically around his neck. I'm sure I was supposed to be intimidated with his athletic prowess, but I had sat through too many of these little headgames with my father to be impressed by this tactic. I stepped out of the shadow and stood motionlessly outside the room, waiting for him to notice me.

It didn't take him more than a minute or two before he spotted me out of the corner of his eye. He gave a little start of surprise and I bit back a smirk. Like Monopoly, this game would be won, not in one bold move, but with a lot of little petty maneuvers. He recovered quickly, wiped the sweat from his forehead, and with a jerk of his head, gestured for me to enter.

I stood where I was, neither openly defying him nor pretending that I didn't understand him. I just stood waiting. After a moment, he shrugged and walked to the door, pulling it open with sarcastic politeness.

"Please, Ms. D'Angelo," he said with an implied bow, "won't you join me?"

I stepped in slowly, looking around as if admiring the facilities. "I'm afraid I'm not dressed for squash."

"Racquetball."

"Same thing." I smiled.

"Not really." I could almost hear his teeth grinding. "Actually, they're very different."

"Oh, that's right," I agreed. "Racquetball has more syllables."

This might sound like pretty banal banter, but actually we were playing a game more aggressive than killer handball. And, go figure, I think I just won that round, but I doubt I would have been that cocky if I hadn't known that Tino, Julie and half the Boston Police Department were within earshot.

O'Halloran tugged on the towel around his neck as if it were the reins attached to his temper. It took him a moment to regain some self-control. He smiled politely, turned and walked towards a blank wall on the other side of the court.

He reached out to push a small recessed handle that blended in perfectly with the wall. A barely detectable pocket door slid back and into the wall, revealing a room beyond. He stood by the doorway, gesturing into the room, his half smile leering at me and his eyes challenging me, daring me to call his bluff or fold.

Under normal circumstances there would be no force on earth powerful enough to get me to go into that room. Usually, I'm not that stupid. However, I was feeling rather like Wonder Woman, wearing pink and green plaid instead of red, white and blue, wired with a G.P.S. transmitter instead of a magic lasso and protected by a Kevlar vest instead of bulletproof bracelets. That aura of invincibility clung to me and I met his leer and raised him a pfft. I walked past him into the inner room.

It was a small room. No windows, but that didn't surprise me since I suspected we were three stories underground. It was decorated very tastefully in tans, browns and hunter green. A huge flat screen television covered one wall with a state of the art theater sound system. Two chairs, a couch and a coffee table took up most of the space in the middle of the room. A small wet bar ran along the back wall. I passed on the couch and sat on one chairs.

"A private little lounge hidden behind a sliding door off the racquetball court," I said conversationally. "Why is it I doubt you've ever met with your board of directors here?"

"You'd be wrong," he said as headed for the wet bar. "Several of the directors are extremely attractive."

He handed me a bottle of water and took the seat across from me. The bottle was cold and the seal was unbroken. Real bottled water. No way could this man be a murderer. I open the bottle and took a deep swig. Sweet. I released a totally sincere sigh of bliss.

"You're a cheap date." He seemed amused.

"Long story," I replied. "Another time." Like maybe never.

A silence fell. It was his meeting, let him start.

"I got your responses," he said at last. "All of them."

"Perhaps not as loquacious as your original discoveries, I tend to respond in a slightly more pithy style."

"Pithy? Is that what you call it?" His voice crackled with a vicious edge of anger.

I racked my brains as I mentally reviewed all of my responses. It was as if one of my counter-filings had really pissed him off. I couldn't figure out what I could have written that could get this fierce of a reaction. Not that I felt bad about it. I'd just like to be able to do it again, if needed.

He finished his bottle of water in one long gulp and then crushed the bottle in one hand. Impressive. Not.

"You seem to have recovered from your *bullet wound* very quickly." He paused before sarcastically saying *bullet wound*. I wasn't quite sure what the inference was, but I was surprised he brought it up first.

"Yes, the doctors are very pleased with my recovery, though the police are still looking for the shooter." I said, watching him from the corner of my eye as I idly swished the water bottle.

He leapt violently to his feet.

"Don't fuck with me, D'Angelo!" he bellowed and hurled his water bottle against the wall.

Not quite as dramatic as if it had been glass, but as far as theatrical displays go, it was quite effective. I didn't bother to try to hide my confusion. I couldn't figure out what I had done to push his buttons this far. But he was ripping mad, and I was starting to get more than a little frightened.

"Okay, I don't know what your problem is, but I think I want to leave now." I stood up but was immediately pushed back in to my chair. He had shoved me hard on my right shoulder. The pain was delayed for half a second, but when it did kick in, I choked back a gasp. If O'Halloran noticed my reaction, he probably thought it was just fear. Spots floated in front of my eyes and for a moment or two; I couldn't focusing on what he was saying.

"...back stabbing, lying whore! I've dealt with some foul slimeballs in this business, but you've taken it to an entirely new low."

I watched him in shock as he ranted around the room, slamming walls, tossing anything he could find, breaking a lot of his own toys. It was if he was a really big, really nasty, spoiled toddler.

"Look, O'Halloran," I tried to keep my voice level and ignore the throbbing in my shoulder. "You just overstepped yourself. You knew perfectly well that you should have served Scollari with the Soldiers and Sailors Act notice, but you got greedy. Don't blame me because you stretched it too far. I'm just the one that bagged you on it. If he had gone to any other attorney, they would have seen the same thing."

Suddenly, O'Halloran's nose was in my face. I pressed myself back into the chair. He wheezed like a bull and his breath smelled of scotch.

"That might be so," he said, his voice low with malice, "but calling the police on me, trumping up this joke of an assault charge, faking your own shooting. I have never come across anyone who was so depraved, so deceitful, so ambitious, that they would stoop that low."

I was speechless. He actual thought I faked the entire shooting. Did he think the police were that stupid that they wouldn't check to see if I'd really been shot? Or did he think that I'd shot myself as part of some convoluted power ploy?

If I wasn't staggered enough by that last statement, his next words left me completely stunned.

"By god, you make me hot!" He grabbed a handful of my hair and pulled my head back. I opened my mouth to protest and hadn't even taken a breath yet when he latched his mouth onto mine in a gesture that was far too violent to be called a kiss. I squirmed to get free, but all that did is to make him shift his weight down on top of me. He leaned on my shoulder and the pain was so blinding that I almost blacked out.

Now would be a good time for the cavalry to arrive.

I tried to kick out at him but couldn't get any leverage with my legs. My right arm was even more useless than it had been earlier, but with my left hand I scratched at his face and pulled at his hair.

With a bellow like a rutting ox, he jerked his face away from mine. His eyes glittered with some kind of animal bloodlust and his grin was all the more gruesome by the blood and scratches on his cheeks. I took a deep breath and let loose with a scream so loud that it hurt my throat. He watched me unblinking until I exhausted my breath. Then he smiled down at me, his eyes not fully focused.

"I love it when they scream," he whispered as if to himself.

Cavalry now, please.

An ungentle yank and I heard the buttons of the jacket rattle to the floor. O'Halloran's hand went to grab at my chest, but suddenly froze.

"What the fuck?" He muttered as he felt the Kevlar vest. He bounced back off me and looked down at my shirt. "What is that? You got some kind of skin condition?"

I didn't speak. I don't think I could have even if I knew what to say. My breath heaved and my vision faded in and out.

I heard the rip of material as he tore open my blouse, exposing the vest beneath.

"What is that? Some kind of chastity belt?"

My vision was clearing but my mind was still foggy. Didn't O'Halloran have a white shirt on? Why is it red now? I saw his gaze follow my eyes down to his chest and his response was immediate.

"Ugh! Blood!" He screamed like an old lady. He ran to the mirror that was over the wet bar. "You bitch! You must have stabbed an artery when you scratched me!"

I could hear the water running in the sink as he washed his face and hands. I pushed myself back up to a sitting position and looked down at the once glorious pink and green plaid suit, now ripped and drenched in blood.

"I don't think it's your blood." I don't know how he heard me, I could barely speak.

"Yuck! Why are you bleeding? You don't have any diseases or anything, do you?"

I pulled myself to my feet. The cavalry wasn't coming. I needed to get out of here.

I hadn't taken my first step towards the door, when it exploded inwards. Two cops, in complete SWAT gear, rushed in and behaved just like on T.V. I was still bleeding and my vision was shaky, but what I could see was beautiful. They made O'Halloran lie face down and put his hands behind his head. His lips moved but I couldn't hear what he was saying. I smiled anyway. I'm sure he was being very polite. I felt someone grab my arm. It was the cavalry. Tino and Julie. Their lips were moving too, but nothing was coming out. I smiled at them. Then the room got very white.

CHAPTER THIRTY

Our mother died when I had just turned eight and Julie was six.

Mama was like a bright pastel scarf being tossed around by a strong wind. She would fly in, caress us both, call us her angels and fly out the door again with a kiss and a giggle and a wave good bye. I remember the way her fingers would glide through my hair and over my cheek. We adored our mother and we always looked with anticipation whenever the wind would blow open the door, hoping it was her. Mama's breeze was better than Christmas.

If Mama was the wind, than Nana, my father's mother, was a rock. Solid as a stone and as constant as the earth beneath your feet, she was there, day and night, providing food and structure and a cold, dour love that paled besides Mama's tempest.

Mama dressed in the brightest of colors. Nana wore black or brown or gray.

Mama would sneak into our school on a warm spring morning to steal us away so that we could spend the afternoon playing hookey on the Cape.

Nana would bring us to church every Sunday.

Mama would take us shopping and buy us fantastic gowns and frivolous dresses that would stay in our closets until we outgrew them because there wasn't one place on God's green earth where little girls could wear those kinds of dresses.

Nana made sure that we had plenty of clean underwear and warm socks to go with our Catholic school uniforms.

Mama was tall and blonde and willowy, like Julie. But if Julie is like Mama, than I'm like Nana, and that is not a happy thought.

I think I turned into Nana that year that we lost them both. Nana's death was really hard for me. Julie had just turned six and was more puzzled by her disappearance than upset.

"Your Nana's gone to heaven to be with God" the nuns told me. I didn't blame God for that. He probably need clean socks and hot pasta too.

And for a few glorious months, Mama was there. Every day. We'd come home from school and she was there. The food wasn't as good as Nana's, it was usually takeout. And the house wasn't as clean as Nana kept it, but it had Mama. I missed Nana, but for a few glorious months, every day was Christmas because Mama was there.

Then one day, we ran up the stairs and the house was empty. I had never seen the house empty before. We ran from room to room, calling for her, but there was no one there. I remember how our voices echoed. They had never echoed like that before.

Then Papa came home and told us that Mama had gone to heaven to be with God. I think I blamed

God a lot more for that one. I mean, Mama was a real lousy cook and He had Nana. What did He need Mama for?

Papa said that Mama had died from an embolism. I thought he said that she had died from an ambulance and to this day I am still deathly afraid of sirens.

✢

Pitiful. The ride from Government Center to Mass General Hospital is actually shorter than the trip to the police station, and despite the fact that I was weak from shock and blood loss, they still had to restrain me in the ambulance.

Ambulances completely freak me out.

My "meeting" with O'Halloran had popped four stitches and re-opened a partially healed artery. Three hours later, I was restitched, my fluids topped off, and once more seated in the front passenger seat of the venerable Lincoln Towncar, Tino behind the wheel, and Julie in the back. The pink and green suit lay in state in the trunk, wrapped up in a plastic bag, and I wore a light blue jogging suit that Julie had bought at the hospital gift shop. It was plastered all over with the words "Mass General Hospital." The way the last week or so had been going, it was only right that I should be a walking advertisement for emergency rooms everywhere.

I had barely touched vinyl when I asked the million dollar question: "Where were you guys?"

Silence reigned for a moment or two. Tino's face was redder than normal, a vein pulsing above his jaw which he clenched tightly. I turned to look at Julie.

"We couldn't find you," she admitted sheepishly.

"What?"

It was Tino who answered. "The lowest level wasn't supposed to be open. It never got its building department approvals and the emergency exits were sealed. The only way down there was by the elevator and that floor was locked out. No one in O'Halloran's office claimed to have a key."

"Elf-boy had it," I offered, a little late for that information.

"The avocado tooth fairy?" asked Julie.

"I thought it was more of a mint green," I said.

"Have you ever seen a more disgusting office?" Julie's voice echoed my own contempt.

"I know!" I agreed. "It was like---"

"Ladies?" Tino seemed a tad bemused. "The point?"

"The point," Julie explained, as if she were talking to a three year old, "is that someone in O'Halloran's office has very bad taste."

"To say the least," I added.

Tino shook his head and then continued. "Well, we were at a bit of a stalemate, until Julie stepped in." Tino glanced in the rear view mirror as if to share a private laugh with Julie. I looked down to see my hands clutched into tight fists. I made a conscious effort to straighten my fingers.

"Well, the police were going to wait until the fire department showed up with the pass key!" said Julie as if this excused all. "So I took matters into my own hands."

Despite the pain in my shoulder, I turned in my seat to face Julie. She had that contrite look on her face that she got when she was about to apologize for doing something completely outrageous.

"What did you do?" I asked in a voice of long-suffering.

"I grabbed Teeny's gun and stuck it right in the tooth fairy's business! Told him I'd blow his little joystick into spam if he didn't unlock the elevator!"

I felt the blood drain from my face. The idea of Julie holding a gun was enough to make me see spots. The visual of her pointing a loaded gun at anyone, even the sniffling little elf-boy was terrifying. I turned glazed eyes towards Tino.

"The safety was on," he said, as if that made it all right.

"So, he says 'you wouldn't dare, not in front of all these cops!'" Julie continued, her eyes sparkling. "There were about four police officers standing there, and they all just looked at each other, then turned their backs on us and started looking at pictures on the wall! It was so funny!"

I really wasn't strong enough yet to deal with this.

"So, I said 'it's not like you use it,' and he looked at me, all hissy-spit, and said 'Sweet thing, I use it all the time, I just don't waste it on euro-trash like you.'"

Julie chuckled. She had the strangest sense of humor.

"Then he swished a path to the elevator, waved his magic wand and when we pushed the elevator button for "C" it finally stayed lit." Julie said. "There were six of us jammed into that little elevator, Teeny and I and four S.W.A.T. cops. It was, um, cozy."

"Then, we had a little trouble finding the room you were in," Tino admitted.

"I had said, out loud, that it was a hidden room behind the racquetball court, didn't you hear me?"

Tino looked even more uncomfortable. I glanced back at Julie, who was suddenly intent on pushing back her cuticles.

"What?" I tried very hard to keep all the apprehension I was feeling out of my voice. I have no idea how successful I was.

"The, um, bug stopped working," Julie muttered.

"WHAT?"

"It was a BPD bug," said Tino, referring to the fact that the police department had provided the equipment. "Since they didn't expect you to be going that far down below grade, they used one that had a cleaner frequency at higher elevations. It cut out while you were in the private elevator."

I turned and looked straight out the windshield, my eyes seeing nothing.

"So all the time I was down there, playing frat house football with O'Halloran, I was completely on my own?" My voice sounded like it was coming from someone else's mouth.

Julie started to answer. She knew that I didn't want the truth. She knew that I really wanted to be lied to. And she, being the good sister that she sometimes is, was ready to oblige.

Tino, on the other hand, having this mistaken belief that honesty is the best policy, jumped in.

"Yes."

I did not want to hear that. I sat there wondering if I could force myself to pretend that I never heard that.

"C'mon," said Tino at last. "Let's go."

I finally noticed that we had been parked for a few minutes without moving. I looked out the window, trying to get my bearings.

"Where?" I asked.

"Police Department." Tino answered. "O'Halloran's under arrest, but they don't know what to charge him with until you file your statement."

I looked over at Tino. He got out without meeting my eyes and walked around the car. He opened both mine and Julie's doors, and waited.

Note to self: Next time I suggest spending the day hiding under the bed, do it.

CHAPTER THIRTY-ONE

I woke groggy from a hot, dead sleep; the kind that is so heavy and sultry, you can barely breathe. I kicked off the blanket threatening to suffocate me and stared blankly up at an unfamiliar ceiling as I tried to recover my bearings.

The ceiling was made of antique tin tiles, the intricate details of its filigree blunted by layers of dust and ivory paint. The etched glass ceiling-mounted light fixture was turned off. What light there was in the darkened room came from a small dim window mounted high on the wall and from the other side of a frosted pane of glass that was set in the only door. I sat up, wiped the crud out of my eyes, and looked around.

I lay on a long black leather couch, well-worn like someone had been sleeping on it pretty regularly for more than a couple of years. Shelves of books took up most of the walls. A large oak desk dominated the room. It was a battered craftsman-era antique and it reminded me of the desks in Tino's office.

With a start, I glanced back to the door and realized that I must be in Tino's inner office. Last thing I recalled, I was giving a statement to McBeige at the police station. McBeige and Tino had left the room for a moment, and I'd put my head down on the table to close my eyes for a moment.

Next thing I remember, I'm waking up on this sofa.

I rubbed, I scratched, I sniffed, I shook the last bit of sleep out of my head, and I took a good look around the room.

On the walls that weren't covered with bookshelves, were hung all kinds of maps: U.S. revolutionary maps, Civil War maps, the Ottomon Empire, as well as current maps. A map of the Mediterranean and Mid-east, mounted on corkboard, had dozens, possibly hundreds, of little colored tacks. I tried to figure out what they could stand for, but I could see no rhyme nor reason to their location.

The books were an eclectic collection of American History, Law Books, sports trivia and gun catalogs. I pulled out a familiar college text book that was sandwiched between a book of essays on the Federalist Papers and a volume of Yogi Berra anecdotes. Phillip had a similar book and the stamp on the flyleaf showed that it had been bought, secondhand, at the Northeastern University Bookstore. I replaced it on the shelf, figuring that Tino must have gone to N.U. for Criminal Justice. A lot of cops did that if they wanted to make detective.

I was no more than mildly curious about the papers cluttered on the desk and I hope I would have never have been so rude as to pry if I hadn't picked up my own name on top of the one of the piles. It was the police report from that afternoon, a transcript of my version of the morning's events with a note on the bottom stating that the remainder of the debriefing had to be postponed due to the witness (that would be me) being unable to continue after taking pain medication that rendered her unconscious.

Yeah, like in my condition I'm supposed to keep track of which pills are for day use and which ones are for night time.

The page had a small red "f" written in the upper right corner, so I figured Tino meant to file it. I wasn't being nosy, I was just being helpful, but I will admit that I was more than a little curious as to what else might be in his "file" on this case.

I noiselessly opened the top drawer, then blew whatever delusions of stealth I might have had by squeaking in surprise. I will never get used to the idea of people leaving guns around in drawers. It was a Glock 9mm semi, probably the same one that Julie had used to ventilate the filing cabinets. I picked it up carefully. It was fully loaded. I popped out the clip, cleared the chamber and checked the barrel. It was filthy. Unlocked, fully loaded and dirty taboot. I shook my head. How can a person treat a gun so carelessly?

I took it in my hand and felt its heft. I sighted it and played with the action. Not bad, but I don't like Glocks. They seem more like weapons than guns. I stopped mid-thought.

That didn't even make sense to me.

Repressing the urge to find a cleaning rod and some rags, I reloaded the gun and replaced it in the drawer. Nothing else of interest in the top drawer: pens, pencils, letter opener, odd keys, bullets of almost every caliber, even a couple of spent shells. Maybe he kept those for sentimental reasons. The mind balked at trying to figure out what he had used the bullets for that he would hang on to the empty shells.

The next couple of drawers were only slightly interesting. Beyond the normal pads of paper and assorted office supplies, he had an entire drawer full of electronic doo-dads, most of which I couldn't begin to tell you what they might be. A couple looked like the G.P.S. devices and the listening bugs that I had used earlier. There were a lot of jumbled cables and wires and my fingers itched to unravel them and wrap them neatly into tight little bundles.

The bottom drawer was file-sized and I ran my fingers over the tabs to scan the contents. Unfortunately, Tino's system of organized chaos did not include labeling. I pulled out the front four files.

Each of the folders was between two and three inches thick. The first two were full of printouts from the same source, stapled together in neat stacks. The last two were a hodgepodge of reports, clippings, photos, receipts and odd documents. I opened the first of the print out folders.

When I was a little kid, I had one teacher at St.

Mary's who'd tell us that Archangel Gabriel kept a book of everything we did, good and bad, and that someday, he was going to tell God on us. I always pictured Archangel Gabriel as a smarmy tattletale snoop who wore broken glasses and pants hiked up around his chest. As I looked down at this file, I realized that old Gabe had been moonlighting at Unitech Data Resources, LLC., a personal data broker. And he was thorough.

My school records since first grade, including notes from Sister Beningus. My medical records: I never knew my mother was in labor for sixteen hours and that the delivering physician was Dr. Korjeski. Overdue library books from the eighth grade. Every mention of me in the year book, the school paper and the local paper. I paged through in shock, and then I turned to the next stack.

My SAT scores, Achievement tests, LSATs, Law Boards, all spelled out and analyzed in more detail than even I had given. Every credit card charge, some even with the itemizations of the things that I purchased. Flights I had taken. The top 100 phone numbers that I called each year, with the promise of more details available upon request. My fingers were shaking by the time I made it through the first file.

I felt raped.

The second file was on my father. I paged through one or two pages before slamming it shut. I knew all I wanted to know about my father, I did not want to know any of the stolen details that

Gabriel the snitch had compiled over the years.

The building creaked, a motorcycle roared down the street, I paused in my prying to listen, but I couldn't hear anything beyond the usual sounds of the city.

Upstairs, I heard people walking about occasionally, but they might as well have been on another planet, my entire universe was now focused on these file folders.

The third file started out innocuously enough. Photocopies of newspapers clippings, parking ticket printouts, rosters of addresses near the crime scenes; Scollari somehow managed to get a copy of the police report on my father's car accident. I skimmed over it quickly; I didn't want to relive any part of that.

He also had the police reports on the current events. I forced myself to read the police reports on Lucy Rudd's murder, but found out very little more than what I already knew. I skimmed over the witness statements and the ballistics reports. O'Halloran's alibi was corroborated; he was in a restaurant with a date that night. It was interesting that McAdams had questioned Scollari about his whereabouts, and Julie had been the witness that confirmed that he had been in the North End all evening.

The report on my shooting was equally comprehensive, but less informative, no ballistics reports and while all the witnesses reported hearing the gun shots, no one recalled seeing or hearing a person nor a car leaving the area. Scollari's statement took four pages. McAdams had asked him the same question twelve different ways. O'Halloran's alibi was shaky. Supposedly he was alone with a woman who had an extensive criminal record. A "professional escort", an expensive one too, the report implied.

Reviewing the cold, impersonal police reports had slightly eased my initial feelings of violation, and with a restored calm, I opened the flap on an unmarked manila envelope that was in the file. I pulled out a stack of photocopied reports and once more, my world fell apart.

It was a copy of some report, Xerox copies of photographs, noted with dates and some shorthand codes that meant little to me beyond the fact that I could recognize the initials of the subjects, because I knew the subjects.

I was in almost all of the pictures. And the pictures looked like they had all been taken during my last two summers at the Cape. There were dozens of pictures, possibly more than a hundred of them, all of them taken covertly, with that paparazzi style that made you think of people hiding behind bushes with telescopic lenses.

But who would take pictures of a fifteen year old on summer vacation? And why?

I paged numbly through the pages of the report. There were some pictures of me by myself, one with Dad, a couple with Julie, but most of the pictures were of me with Alex, my boyfriend those two summers. I shook my head to clear the mayhem in my mind. Later, I would try to understand how these fit into the case. Right now, I needed to figure out what these pictures meant and who took them.

And how did they get into Tino's files?

I closed my eyes and took a few deep breaths. Eight second rosary. Three second yoga. Ommmm. Okay. I'm ready.

This time paging through, I forced myself to look past the pictures and focus on the context.

The first picture was of me, walking the beach. It looked like early morning. The notation said "Subject: Josephine D'Angelo, Age 15". Like I needed a note to remind me that I was 15. I had been a late bloomer and that summer, three months short of my sixteenth birthday, I was still flat as a board. Pitiful.

The header stated: CASE #1645224, FILE 14B" and the footer indicated page 118. Why would a boring, flat-chested fifteen year old be included as a part of some other file? And what was that file of? And what kind of pervo had compiled it?

After the first picture, the rest of the notations had just referred to me as "JD". Dad was noted as "JDSR" and Julie was "JD2". She sounded like a character from Star Wars. I paged front and back to see if the report included a key to the abbreviations, but no luck. It must have been included elsewhere in the file. Alex showed up in a lot of the pictures, referred to as "AA2" for Alexander Andrews. Weird. Who was "AA1"? The other notes referred to date and time, in the format of date.month.year, then military time. Then additional gibberish of numbers and letters that may have meant location, but could just as well have meant about anything else too.

For a moment, I lost my fear and anger as I looked at one of the shots of Alex and me. We were out on the boat. (Where the hell was the photographer that he got such a clear shot of us out at sea?) The picture was grainy and badly balanced since it was a photocopy of what looked to have been a color picture, yet, how weird that I could almost recall that exact moment? It was definitely the second summer, since I actually had a small amount of boobage to fill out my bathing suit. Alex's head was turned and I could tell by his expression that he had just said something to tease me, probably about my cleavage since for the first two weeks of our second summer vacation, he rarely mentioned anything else. At the time, I remember thinking that he acted like he was due some kind of credit for the belated arrival of my bustline. He would glance at them and grin and then look around as if he was waiting for someone to congratulate him about them. And whenever we were alone, he managed to work some kind of implied comment about them into almost every sentence he said. And I would inevitably respond by smacking him on the back of his head.

I ran my fingertip over the hazy image of his face. It was funny how golden your first "puppy love" could seem in retrospect.

I pulled myself back from wondering about whatever might have happened to Alex. I replaced the report into the envelope and put it back into the file. I would have liked to have taken them all with me, but I didn't want Tino to know that I had seen them. I was reaching for the fourth file when I heard some noise in the outer office. Quickly, I replaced the files, quietly closed the drawer, and went back to lie on the couch.

A Tino-sized silhouette appeared on the other side of the frosted window door and slowly and silently began to open the door. He was quietly standing in the doorway when the street door behind him opened and slammed shut. He spun around and went back into the outer office, closing the door behind him.

I sat up and listened intently. It was too quiet for too long out there. And nothing peaceful about that silence. I could feel the tension right through the door and it was smothering.

"Scollari." I recognized that voice. It was O'Halloran and he was nearly stuttering with fury. I hugged the blanket to my chest as if that would give me an extra layer of protection against his venom.

"Made bail?" Tino didn't really ask that, it was more of a taunt.

"Easy enough, since the so-called *victim* never bothered to complete her statement to the police."

"Funny that the judge just didn't dismiss the charges outright, considering that the victim was unconscious in I.C.U." Tino's voice was so emotionless that it made you think twice to catch the sarcasm.

"This is a crock of shit and you know it! That whore set the whole thing up!"

There was a quick sharp thud, then a rather satisfying crash. It sounded like someone just decked someone else and I really hoped that O'Halloran was getting his own blood all over his shirt this time. Another long pause, but this time I heard panting and the rustle of somebody getting back up to their feet. Then silence.

"I don't think I understood you," said Tino quietly after a moment. "Maybe you can try that again without the color commentary."

I really was enjoying this much too much. I only wish I could see what was going on. I stood up and walked to the door so that I could hear better.

"I know what you two are up to. She's good, I'll give you that. And she's got that wide-eyed innocent routine down to a science. But she's a player, like her father was. Maybe even worse than D'Angelo. D'Angelo fooled no one with his games. But she's got you and the entire Boston Police Department dancing like a pack of trick bears. But I'm warning you, Scollari. Watch your back."

I felt like someone just punched me in the gut. I never had the least desire to be a wheeler-dealer like Dad. I always let Uncle Benny handle all that stuff because I just didn't have the stomach for it. Now, just because I didn't back down, he thinks I'm a player too.

Or was it that I *couldn't* back down? After all, I *am* Joe D'Angelo's daughter. As much as I hate all the stress of those conflicts, it never occurred to me to quit or back off. Maybe I *am* a bit of a Spartan gladiator as well.

The hush in the outer office lasted no more than a few seconds.

"Did you come here to give me this friendly advice, or is there actually some intelligent reason for your visit?" Tino's voice was casual and friendly. It reminded me a bit of Dad, just before he swooped in for the kill.

"I've got a proposition for you," O'Halloran said after another pause. "If the c..., If Ms. D'Angelo drops the assault and battery charges, I'll drop the default litigation against you."

Tino snorted in disgust. "I doubt---"

"We accept," I said quietly, stepping through the door into the outer office.

Tino spun around to face me, his eyes narrowing. I looked past him, to O'Halloran, who, after a moment's surprise, schooled his expression into a disrespectful sneer.

I was disappointed to see no blood on his jacket, but he did have a lovely bruise on his jaw. He looked me up and down and I realized, belatedly, how it must look. Tino had appeared to have been coming out of the inner office, and now I came out of that same room, looking rumpled and tousled as if I just got out of bed, but not from sleeping. I restricted myself to a mental shrug, ignored Tino's eyes and met O'Halloran's glare.

"You withdraw the liability suit against Scollari, and I won't press assault and battery charges."

O'Halloran's glare morphed into a resigned leer and he stepped past Tino to stand inches in front of me. Really, the man had some definite personal space issues. After a moment, he pulled out a white envelope from his jacket pocket and, without breaking eye contact, he reached behind him to drop it on the nearest desk.

"That's *one*, D'Angelo," he said ambiguously.

I had no idea what he meant by that, so I said nothing and waited. When it became obvious that I wasn't going to respond, he reached out, flicked a lock of hair off my forehead, and turned and walked to the door.

Turning back, he glanced at me again, then he looked over at Tino.

"Remember what I said," he warned. "Watch your back with this one."

He left much more quietly than he entered.

Tino's breath was almost hissing he was so angry. I raised my eyebrows, silently questioning him as to what his temper was about. He walked to the desk, picked up the envelope, and ripped it into pieces without even opening it.

I sighed and shook my head. It was a brilliantly dramatic gesture, but pretty meaningless. The paperwork was not as important as the intent. I knew that O'Halloran could reinstate his claim against Scollari anytime within seven years of the default, and O'Halloran knew he could still be threatened by my charges anytime within the statute of limitations. What we had was a détente and it didn't need that paperwork to be in effect.

"You do realize that your little stunt isn't legal!" Tino's bellow rattled the glass in door. "Why would you let him off the hook? How do you know that he wasn't the one who shot you at the beach? How do you know he didn't kill Lucy Rudd?"

Tino's voice turned cold and ominous. "You just let a possible murderer and rapist buy his freedom. Is that what they teach you in that fancy law school?"

I stepped back from his anger; I hadn't retreated from O'Halloran, but Scollari's fury unsettled me. I could feel the blood draining from my face.

"O'Halloran had alibis for both assaults." My voice sounded reedy in my ears. "You didn't hear him in the gym this morning. He thought I had contrived my own shooting. I told you from the start, I didn't think it was him. Your property is definitely worth going after, but it's not worth killing someone for."

"How about his assault on you? That wasn't just an innocent business meeting. He's done that before and he's got away with it."

"And did you see what his attorneys did to that woman?"

"So you admit that you're backing off because you're afraid of him?"

"Grow up, Scollari!" I lost my temper and yelled my throat hoarse. "If we had met him in court over the broken lease, he may have very well have got a judgment for the full amount, plus additional damages. And if I pressed charges for assault, his attorney would have asked me one very important question. Would I have gone with him into that room if I wasn't under the mistaken impression that I had the entire Boston Police Department wired into my pocket! And the answer would be no, there's no way I would have even shown up this morning if I hadn't been pushed into it by you and the police. Can you spell 'entrapment'? His attorneys would argue that O'Halloran had made a reasonable assumption as to my willingness because of my actions."

"You nearly bled to death!" He roared at me.

"Because he didn't believe I had a gunshot wound," I yelled back at him. "My walking in less than a week after the shooting looking like a spring flower in that obscene suit probably just reinforced his belief that I had made up the whole thing." I dropped my voice down, mostly because my throat hurt too much to yell any more. "Trust me, O'Halloran just paid a lot more for his 'crime' than the legal system would have cost him."

I forced myself not to flinch away as Scollari's eyes scorched into mine.

"I don't like the idea of you being beaten bloody as an exchange for getting me out from under a bad business decision."

"Okay, so that's the problem." I rolled my eyes. "It's not about justice or morality. It's about your pride."

Tino opened his mouth to argue with me, but I cut him off.

"Listen. Given the choice, I would rather go nose to nose with O'Halloran in the courtroom rather than the E.R., but since I've already gotten beaten to a pulp, we might as well make the most of it. If I can avoid going two more rounds with O'Halloran in the courtroom, once for your litigation and the other time for the criminal assault charge, then call me a coward, 'cause I'm taking the easy way out."

"So I suppose I shouldn't even bother getting the rest of your statement?" asked McBeige's voice.

Tino and I whipped around to see McBeige, replete with tan trench coat, standing next to the closed door. I hadn't heard the door open nor had I seen him enter. I glanced up to see if there was a trap door in the ceiling he might have fallen through.

"When did you get here?" asked Tino sharply.

"Never mind that," I said. "*How* did he get in here?"

McBeige smiled slightly while I scoped out the furniture near him to see if he might have been hiding behind it all this time. I would have bet my last meatball that he couldn't have come through that door without my seeing him.

"I came to get the rest of Ms. D'Angelo's

statement." McBeige chose to ignore both our questions. "But I guess I have to tell Hatteras that we won't be pressing charges?"

Since I didn't know how much McBeige had heard, I started to explain, but he lifted his hand to stop me until he had pulled out his little tape recorder. We ended up back in Tino's inner office and I recapped for the two of them everything that had happened in the little room behind the racquetball court. Tino was even more silent than usual. He stood in the doorway with his arms crossed, not moving. If he wasn't so big, I'd accuse him of sulking. I stopped short of recapping the deal O'Halloran and I had made, but evidently McBeige had heard enough of my and Tino's conversation, because when I was done, he shut off the recorder with a snap and looked thoughtfully off into space for a moment.

"You were right," he said finally. "I'm not completely eliminating O'Halloran as a suspect in either the murder or your shooting, but based on what you're saying happened in the health club, the worse he might have received would have been a suspended sentence. And with his attorneys, he probably would have got off scot-free."

I refrained from sticking my tongue out at Tino, but my look said it all.

✑✑

CHAPTER THIRTY-TWO

McBeige's trenchcoat had just disappeared up the stairs to the street when Julie walked in, a covered plate that smelled of hot pasta in her hands, and that expression of cheerful apology on her face that I feared so much.

"Oh dear God, now what?" I asked resignedly. Guilty smiles and peace offerings dripping with tomato sauce are never good omens. "What did you do?"

She placed the plate down on the desk and uncovered it. Spaghetti with meatballs, it smelled heavenly. My stomach rumbled gratefully which completely undermined my intention to glare at her until she confessed. I unwrapped the fork and napkin and dived in. I figured I would need my strength to deal with whatever Julie had been up to.

"Well, you know what Tino said about 'eliminating' suspects?" she asked.

"Mm-hmmm," My mouth was full so all I could do was nod.

"Well, I decided to eliminate a suspect." Julie eyed me hesitantly.

I chewed, swallowed, wiped my mouth and looked her in the eye. "Which one and how?" I don't think I was out of line to be a little wary.

"I called Uncle Benny," she said in a rush. "I told him I'm voting to sell the Raleigh Street property."

My face felt numb. I looked at her without blinking. Tino watched me closely. Julie must have already told him because he didn't seem surprised by her bombshell.

"You can't!" I stuttered at last. "Daddy said--"

"Listen, Jo!" Julie cut me off. "The reason why Daddy made you a trustee was so that you could make these kinds of decisions. Daddy wasn't some oracle. He didn't know he was going to die when he did, he couldn't know about this offer, and he sure as hell didn't know someone was going to start shooting at you. You can't look at his instructions like they're the tablets from Mount Sinai."

I don't what surprised me more, that Julie was actually taking an active interest in the business or that her opinion showed an unexpected maturity. I had too many things bouncing around in my brain. I opened and closed my mouth like a beached carp.

"Jo, I really don't care about the money," she went on. "I know that scares you, but there are days that I wish that I didn't have two cents that I didn't earn myself. And I certainly don't think that Dad's money is worth you dying for."

"So what you're saying is that you think it *was* Uncle Benny that shot me?"

"Noooo," she drew out the syllable scornfully. "But if there is another attempt, at least we can pretty much eliminate Uncle Benny as a suspect."

I didn't want to think about another attempt. I stared at the corner of the desk, my eyes not focusing. It had been a bad day. A long, bad, scary, painful and confusing day. And it wasn't even full dark yet. I needed everything to slow down for a while. I needed time to think.

"Eat your spaghetti…" Tino said quietly.

I looked up to see Tino watching me closely, wearing his stone face.

"…and I'll drive you home."

CHAPTER THIRTY-THREE

There was very little conversation on the ride back to Cohasset. Those photographs in Tino's files were boggling me. Could the current murder attempts be related to something that happened ten years ago? I couldn't think of one thing that happened during those two summers that could have possibly been of any interest to anyone but me.

I don't know why I didn't want to discuss those photos with Tino. Some instinct told me not to trust him, but since I couldn't think about anything else, I said almost nothing all the way home.

"I'll stay here tonight," said Julie, her voice unusually subdued as we pulled into the driveway.

I mumbled some response, still absorbed in my own thoughts and got out of the car. I hadn't even taken a step towards the house when Tino grabbed my arm, pulling me back sharply.

"Don't be such a bitch," he hissed in my ear. "She did what she thought was best for you."

Startled out of my funk, I looked up at him, perplexed. Then I glanced over at Julie, looking quietly miserable by the gate.

"Oh, Ju!" I said. "I'm not pissed about the Raleigh Street thing. Hell, I haven't even started to think about that mess yet! Dad didn't want it sold so soon, but you've got the right to vote anyway you want to."

I hip checked the car door to close it and then collapsed against the hood, massaging my temples with my fingertips. "To tell you the truth, it wasn't until today that it really sunk in that someone *is* actually trying to kill me. Deep down, I think I was hanging on to that slim hope that the shooting down by the breakwater was random; some anonymous maniac emptying a clip into the surf. And that Lucy Rudd's murder wasn't connected to me at all."

I looked past Julie, my eyes unfocused on the deck stairs.

"I don't know if I should walk into that house and never come out until they find the killer, or if I should slap on the Kevlar vest and run up and down Route 93 with a firing range target hung around my neck.

"On one hand," my voice snagged unexpectedly. I took a deep breath and continued, "I don't want to victimize myself by letting this fear control my life. Then again, I really don't want to die just yet either."

My eyes were dry but I wiped them with the heel of my palm anyway. I walked past Julie who still stood by the open gate.

"I think I just need a little time to think."

∽ঔৈ৵

I lay in bed, staring at the ceiling, listening to Julie's and Ant Bee's voices filter up the stairs. I racked my brain, dredging up every stray memory from those summers, but couldn't think of one thing that stuck out as being unusual. At least not to anyone else except me.

I supposed it was a bit strange how I'd met Alex. It was a little before dawn on a misty June morning. I was still a few months short of my sixteenth birthday but Dad had bought me a little catamaran sailboat as an early birthday present and I was out practicing, tacking back and forth off shore. It was a tricky little skiff, and I used the privacy of the pre-sunrise surf to get the hang of it. I still hate it when people watch me when I'm learning something new.

I had been practicing steering from one buoy to another when I noticed some flotsam some ways off. It wasn't until I had tacked right up to it that I discovered that it was a person, a man, clinging to a couple of lobster trap buoys. I managed to pull him onto the boat without capsizing it, not an easy thing to do in a little catamaran.

I would later find out that he was seventeen, about two years older than me. At that moment, however, all I noticed that he was possibly the hottest looking boy that I had ever seen in real life. He had sun-bleached blond hair and all he wore were cutoff jeans. I didn't spend much time admiring his tan, though. He wasn't moving and his skin was icy cold to the touch. I slid my hand under his neck, tilted his head back, and then froze.

It had been more than two years since we covered mouth-to-mouth resuscitation in Girl Scouts and, at that particular moment, I just couldn't remember what to do next.

"Crap!" I muttered. "I forgot how!"

"Oh, give it a try. I bet we can improvise something."

I squeaked and sprung back. I was so startled by the talking corpse that I dropped his head. It thudded against the deck with a sound like a dropped bowling ball.

"Ow!" he said, rubbing the back of his skull.

"You're not dead!" I am so perceptive about those kinds of things.

"Not at the moment, but I might be hemorrhaging internally from a head wound."

Carefully, I lifted his head up again and felt along the back of his scalp. I could feel the lump growing. Gently, I lowered his head back down onto the deck.

"Nope." I lied. "Nothing."

His fingers felt the back of his head and found my fib. He looked up at me and laughed, but then stopped suddenly.

"My legs!" His hand fumbled down and patted his thighs. "I can't feel my legs!"

I prodded his calf with my finger. "You can't feel that?"

"No." He sounded worried. "Try rubbing my

feet. See if that helps."

I moved down to his legs and started chaffing his feet between my hands. They were ice cold, faintly blue and puckered like raisins.

"Is this helping?"

"A little," he said weakly. "Maybe if you rubbed the calves as well."

Give me a break. I was only fifteen and I'd gone to an all-girl Catholic school. I was well above the knees before I realized that, whatever condition that his legs might have been in, the rest of his appendages were working just fine.

"You jerk!" Using my bare feet, I tried to push him off the boat, but even though he was laughing so hard he could barely breathe, he managed to grab the rigging and stay on board.

"No, wait!" His words came out between choppy gasps. "I'm sorry! I couldn't resist!"

Okay, so it was kind of funny. I bit back a smirk and glared at him.

"What are you doing out here in the middle of the ocean?" I asked. We were only about a half mile off shore, but it wasn't an easy swim, either in or out.

"I went for a swim last night and got pulled out by the undertow." He was looking around at the gear on the deck. I figured he probably needed a blanket, so I reached into the hold and pulled one out from the emergency kit.

"By yourself?" I asked as I handed him the blanket. "That was dumb."

He broke off any demonstration of gratitude to shoot me a dirty look. I don't think he was used to having people tell him that he'd acted stupidly, but after a moment, he shrugged and smiled.

"Suppose it was," he said.

We talked as I sailed him back into the dock and we waited for his ride. He laughed at almost everything I said, which might have been gratifying if I'd been trying to be funny. As it was, I felt pretty stupid and lame.

"Look at that!" I pointed at a long black Humvee that pulled into the marina parking lot. It was the first time I had seen ever seen a stretch Hummer. "That has got to be the ugliest car I've ever seen."

I suppose it was inevitable that the car would stop directly in front of us. A pale bald man in a black suit and tie jumped out and ran around the car to open the back door closest to us. I buried my face in my hands as I realized I had just insulted the family car.

I heard Alex chuckle. "I call it the Imperial Cruiser," he whispered. "They have no idea what I'm talking about."

I uncovered my eyes to see a whippet thin woman dethroning from the car. She had a tight cap of platinum blonde hair sculpted close to her head and her face had that wind tunnel look like she'd gone to the plastic surgeon just one time too often. Without speaking a word or even glancing at me, she grabbed Alex by the neck and dragged him into the car. The eunuch chauffeur slammed the door behind them, eyed me for a moment without interest, and then walked around to the driver's side. As the Imperial Cruiser pulled away, the rear window slid down and I saw Alex roll his eyes in a wordless apology. Then the window rose up again.

I hadn't expected to see him again, but later that afternoon, he dropped in at the Clam Shack where everyone hung out. All that summer, he'd show up and we'd sit around and talk.

I never went to his house and rarely saw any of his family. That might seem strange, but at the time we were just kids hanging out at the beach for the summer. Family and school were those foreign things from some other planet that we rarely talked about.

At the end of that August, we exchanged phone numbers and addresses. Alex went to a boarding school in Switzerland. Académie de Mont Saint Blanc or something like that. We wrote occasionally and he even called two or three times. I never called him though; I didn't want to have to explain a transatlantic call to my father. It wasn't a big deal; we didn't really get serious until our second summer.

That second summer, we were inseparable. We were magic. We were the embodiment of all passion, romance and true love. Okay, maybe we were just hormonal, but at the time you couldn't tell us that anyone had ever felt like we did that summer.

And when that summer was over, we separated with promises to call and write. Alex was going to the University of Paris and he promised to get me his phone number and address as soon as he got there.

He never did.

A month later, I got the lamest "maybe-we-can-just-be-friends" letter ever written in the history of relationships. I'm not exaggerating: typewritten with no return address. Even if I wanted to be pathetic and stalk him, he didn't even give me the chance. The depth of my depression was epic, with the result being Phillip Gorson.

If those old photographs were related to the current murder attempts, then maybe it wouldn't hurt to find out whatever happened to Alex and see if he might know what's going on. I rolled out of bed, tiptoed down the stairs and walked into the study, closing the door behind me.

Do you have any idea how many "Alexander Andrews" there are on the internet? Not to mention "Alex Andrews". I tried filtering it by "University of Paris" and "Académie de Mont St. Blanc" but no luck. After three eye-scorching hours of googling, I admitted defeat. Wherever Alex had disappeared to, he had done it well.

It was entirely possible that the photos in Tino's file were unrelated to Alex. It was also possible that they weren't even connected to the murder investigation. Yet I needed to know more about where they had come from and why they were there. Since I wasn't going to admit that I'd been through his files, I couldn't just ask Tino about the pictures. There was no other way. I was going to have break in to Tino's office.

Oddly enough, I felt strangely excited by the idea, as if I was matching up in some game against Tino. Josephine D'Angelo, the timid little rule follower, was actually considering the felony offense of breaking and entering. The higher stakes of murder and assault faded into the shadows as I felt this strange surge of excitement.

Julie wandered into the study at this point. For a moment she'd been concerned because I wasn't in my bedroom where she thought I'd be.

"Just surfing the web," I said blithely, clearing the current screen. With a few keystrokes I purged my internet history. I certainly didn't suspect Julie of having anything to do with the murder attempts, but I wasn't quite sure that she'd go along with my current schemes. It might have been that I still didn't know how serious her relationship with Tino might be, or it might have been that I was just looking forward to crossing swords with Tino and I didn't want to share.

"Dinner ready yet?" I asked with a smile as I closed the laptop.

CHAPTER THIRTY-FOUR

It was a testament to how desperate I had become. To what depths I had sunk to. Of how far I would go to get the information I wanted.

"No thank you, Mrs. Scollari. I've had plenty."

"Call me Mama! You need to eat more!" Mama Scollari reached over to pinch my cheek. "Why don't you come for dinner more often? Julie we see all the time! Tino! Why don't you bring Jo to dinner?"

Tino shrugged and kept eating. I turned to catch Julie's eye and while I was looking the other way, a phantom backhoe dumped another load of spaghetti on my plate. I stared at it in bemusement as if it were a sign from God, a high carb fleece as it were. I got the message. It was time to make my move.

Down the table, Sandra was loudly given child-rearing suggestions to Stephanie, who listened with a glazed eye façade of attentiveness. Actually, the advice sounded quite rational. I wondered if Sandra ever actually applied any of it to her own barbarian horde. When she broke off her lecture to backhand one of her boys, I turned casually to Tino.

"Tino, I think I left something down in your

office yesterday."

"Really? I didn't see anything down out of place today. What did you lose?" Tino didn't look up as he pushed a wedge of bread through the tomato sauce on his plate.

"Um, nothing important, I think it slipped out of my pocket when I was lying on the couch."

"You were wearing that sweatsuit. It didn't have any pockets."

Do you see what I mean about him being the most annoying human being on the entire planet? Any other man would have just grunted and let me go, but this guy has to make it into the Spanish Inquisition. Fine. I still had a couple of aces to play. I pulled out the "scary woman stuff" card.

"It's, um, just some scary woman stuff," I mumbled sheepishly.

There. It's not pretty, but I had to do it. He made me.

"What kind of woman stuff?"

My jaw dropped open. He was actually questioning the inviolability of scary woman stuff? One of the most hallowed tenets of womanhood? Is he insane? When a woman evokes the sacred term of "scary woman stuff", men have only two options. They can turn bright red and look away as they mutter incoherently, or they can turn stark white, look away, and mutter incoherently. That's it. Unless they're a gynecologist, those are their only two options.

"*Scary* woman stuff," I repeated in a whisper.

"What kind of *scary woman stuff?*" he echoed in his normal volume.

A horrified hush fell over the dinner table. Even little Jenna stopped banging on her plate to turn and stare. Uncle Vinnie pulled a newspaper out of thin air and buried his face behind it. *He* knew the proper response for "scary woman stuff."

Mama Scollari came to the rescue.

"Don't be rude, Tino," she said, leaning over to swat him off the back of his head. "You go ahead Jo. The key's on the hook by the door. The one with the blue yarn."

For a half a moment, I did feel a scrap of remorse. It was a little unscrupulous, but as I glanced back, I caught the hint of a smirk on Tino's face. Maybe not "game-set-match" yet. I'd have to move very quickly.

I found the key as promised and headed out the front door and down the stairs.

CHAPTER THIRTY-FIVE

I locked the door behind me and quickly walked into Tino's office. I left his office door open so I could see if anyone came into the lobby area. I paused only a moment to listen to the sounds of the building before quietly opening the bottom desk drawer.

The files were gone. Conspicuously gone. Their blatant absence gaped at me mockingly. I felt along the bottom of the drawer hoping to find, I don't know what.

Nothing. I closed the drawer and started a systematic search of the desk, the bookshelves and the file boxes that were stacked in the corners.

I worked my way out to the outer office, rifling through the seedy file cabinets. The covert aura of this mission was diminishing at the same rate that my temper was rising. That's why he was so smug upstairs! I slammed the bottom drawer shut and gave it a sharp kick for good measure.

"Is that where you normally leave your scary woman stuff?"

I whirled around to see Tino leaning against the closed door. I hadn't heard him come in.

For a moment I felt a flicker of embarrassment

for being caught snooping, but a good offense is the best defense and I was feeling a little offensive at the moment.

"Where's the file?" I snapped.

"File?" That attitude of feigned innocence was not attractive.

"You know which file." I walked up to him, wishing that someone had had the foresight to leave a stepstool near the door. It's really difficult to intimidate someone who is a good foot taller than you. "My file. The file you compiled on the murder attempts. The file with those pictures of me when I was a teenager. *That* file."

"So you admit that you went through my desk."

"Don't you turn this around on me," I said, neatly deflecting his attack. "I had every right to see that file. It's your fault for not sharing that info with me in the first place."

You like that? Now the whole thing is his fault. Take notes, I'm getting good at this.

"Maybe if you asked nicely?" He leaned down until his nose was within inches of mine.

My molars ached from clenching my jaw. "Please, Mr. Scollari," my voice dripped with saccharine. "May I see that file?"

He stepped away from me and walked over to one of the desks. "No." The tone of his voice was mockingly childish. "It's too late now."

"Give me that file!"

I did not actually stamp my foot, but the tone of my voice had the same effect. In keeping with the current level of maturity, Tino gave me a look equivalent to sticking out his tongue. This conversation was degenerating fast.

I took a deep breath. "Where did those pictures come from?" I asked. "And who took them?"

Tino stared at me for a long moment, the humor fading from his eyes. "They're not connected with the current investigation. You'll just have to trust me on that one."

"Trust you?" I stuttered in disbelief. "Trust you? I barely know you! Within twelve hours of meeting you, a woman is murdered, apparently because of her resemblance to me. I've known you less than two weeks and in that time I've been shot, assaulted, almost raped and practically smothered to death with pasta! And then I discover that you've got a whole bunch of photos of me, taken ten years ago without my knowledge, and you expect me to trust you? How gullible do you think I am?"

I forced myself to meet his eyes as he stared at me stonily. Slowly he walked towards me and I girded myself so I wouldn't back away. Again, he stopped within inches of my face.

"So you don't trust me?" he whispered.

Truth be told, I didn't know if I trusted him or not. Part of me wanted to, it would be so much easier not to have to worry about this mess and dump the whole problem into his lap. Yet somewhere in the back of my head, a loud voice was screaming that there was no logical reason to trust him. And it was that part of my brain that kept me silent.

"Good," he said at last. "Trust should be earned and decisions should be made based on logic, not emotion."

He reached out and gently touched the furrow that rippled between my brows. The tip of his finger lightly traced a route up to my widow's peak and then blazed a feathery trail down my hairline, around my earlobe and along the contour of my jaw. When it reached my chin and began gliding delicately upward, my lips, acting on their own volition, parted expectantly.

"Of course," he whispered, his face leaning even closer to mine, "one shouldn't disregard emotion all together. Emotion can be very important. Sometimes our hearts can see truths that our minds are blind to."

My cardio vascular system staged a swift and bloody coup. The little voice in my head was bound, gagged and shoved into a mental gym locker. Blood was pulsing up and down my arteries like French peasants rioting in the streets outside Versailles. My mind completely stopped working. Chaos ruled.

I rose up on the balls of my feet as I felt his lips brush mine. It was just as the tip of my tongue was gently tasting the roof of his mouth that the nasty little voice of logic broke free.

"SISTER'S BOYFRIEND!" it screamed.

My eyes flew open and for a moment I froze. Then I dropped my head straight down, knocking my forehead against Tino's chin as I dived out of his reach.

"OW!" He grabbed at his jaw. I think he bit his tongue.

I apparated, only to rematerialize on the other side of the room, crouching behind the relative safety of the desk. I stood motionlessly, guilt and lust warring for control. I needed to get out of here. For the first time in my memory, I really thought that guilt was going to lose out. Warily, I watched as Tino slowly turned towards me.

I thought he was going to explode. He stared at me for a long moment and then he started to shake. I backed away, wondering if I could make it out the front door if he went to swing at me.

"Joey," he muttered, his hand moving from his jaw up to cradle his forehead. "If romance were a professional sport, you would be the Boston Red Sox."

I relaxed slightly as I realized that he was laughing, but I wasn't quite sure what he was talking about. I hoped he wasn't talking about stuff like Earned Run Averages or something like that. I didn't want to have to tell him that, notwithstanding this year's pennant chances, I was pretty certain that the Red Sox have scored more often than I have.

"Where did those pictures come from?" I asked. I needed to get back to my comfort zone of homicidal maniacs and pedophile stalkers.

With a sigh of resignation, he leaned against the other desk and crossed his arms.

"When I ran a background check on you, I came across a reference to an old F.B.I. investigation that took place down on the Cape ten years ago. You just happened to be on the periphery of that investigation. They ran surveillance on you as a matter of procedure. They did that on quite a few people that summer. I called in some favors that I have with the F.B.I. and got a copy of that portion of the report that mentioned you. I cross checked all the references and couldn't find anything or anyone that is currently connected to you. It was a dead end."

I watched Tino closely as he spoke. Unfortunately, being such a lousy liar myself, I'm also the easiest person in the world to lie to. He looked sincere, but somehow the whole thing didn't ring true.

"Can I look at the file again?" I asked.

"It's confidential. I'd get my contact in deep trouble if anyone knew I had it."

"Well, since I've already seen it, the confidentiality has been breached."

"I've shredded it."

Okay. I did NOT believe any part of that last statement.

"How about the rest of those files?" I watched him carefully as he thought about how to answer. "You didn't shred the rest of those reports, did you?"

"What do you want to know? I'll pull out what you need."

I was holding on to my temper by the tips of my fingernails. I came out from behind the desk and got right into Tino's face.

"What I want to know," I said slowly, "is who is trying to kill me. And why."

He met my glare but didn't answer. We were still at a standoff when the door opened and Julie walked in.

"Jo?" There were too many questions in Julie's voice to even begin to answer.

Tino and I stayed locked in a face off.

"I want to go home," I said, not even turning to look at her. "Now."

CHAPTER THIRTY-SIX

Julie bore the brunt of my bad mood for the drive home. I had plotted and connived, pulled myself out of my self-imposed seclusion, and then got caught snooping. For what? Nothing. I still didn't know much more about those photographs than I did last night.

Okay, so there was the kiss. But that was as bad as everything else. I looked over at Julie. Was Tino coming on to her as strong as he was coming on to me? How serious was she about him? When we were teenagers and this kind of thing happened, we'd just tossed a coin.

"Julie…" I doubted that this was going to sound as casual as I wanted. "What do you think about Tino?"

Julie turned to me with a huge smile glowing like the headlight of an oncoming train. "Oh Jo! Isn't he the greatest? From the first day I met him, I knew he was a nice guy, and the longer I know him, the more I like him. Don't you?"

Can I just die now? How could I tell her that he'd been coming on to me almost every time we were alone? And that I really liked it? How could I say that, as much as I was attracted to him, I couldn't trust him? How could I tell her that I was certain, at the very least, that he knew some things about this investigation that he wasn't sharing? And that, at the very worst... No, I didn't even want to think about that.

"He's a little annoying." God, I was such a coward.

"No, he's just teasing you! You like him, don't you?"

I could see how important this was to her, and yet, I didn't want to lie to her either. But what did I have beyond some vague suspicions? A mini-orgasm every time I got near him, that's what I had.

"Yeah, I like him." Understatement of the year.

Julie shot me a quick smile as she reached over and squeezed my knee affectionately.

"I knew you would!" she said.

I am going to burn in hell, I just know it.

CHAPTER THIRTY-SEVEN

I couldn't sleep. A four hour Monopoly marathon did nothing to relax me. I was so frazzled that Julie actually beat me. Twice. I was turning into a complete mental defective. What was wrong with me?

Julie had left at midnight, wanting to spend the night at her own apartment in Charlestown. I understood that and it didn't bother me. It was the fact that Tino was now parked in his car across from the driveway that was so disconcerting.

My bedroom faced the beach, Julie's old bedroom faced the street. I found myself sitting in her old room, lights out, staring through the sheers, looking down at the old Lincoln Towncar that was parked in the gloom, well beyond the reach of the nearest streetlight.

I was still ticked at him. A half a dozen times, I grabbed my robe and started down the stairs, intending to let him know what I thought about egotistical Italians who thought that they were the only ones who could handle all the facts; who kept secrets from those people that really needed to know these things; who came on to two sisters at the same time; who could kiss as good as he kissed.

No, maybe it was safer to stay inside.

A rumble of thunder got me out of bed for the umpteenth time. I looked out the window and saw heavy rain clouds masking the stars. A nasty storm was blowing in; should I ask Tino if he wanted to wait it out inside?

I grabbed my robe and ran down the stairs.

"Ha! Caught you!" barked a voice in the dark.

I jumped out of my skin as the living room lights flashed on. Ant Bee stood guarding the front door, her arms crossed under her bust, the fiery gleam of righteous vigilance shining from her eyes.

"Don't think I don't know what you're up to! Don't you think you can lie to me! I will have no going hump in the night!"

I collapsed against the stair rail, my heart nearly exploding from the shock.

"No Ant Bee, you don't understand." I said when I could speak again. "There's a storm coming and I just wanted to see if he wanted to wait inside."

"Any sport in a storm? Eh? No, No, No, I think no! He stays outside! You stay inside!"

"At least let me bring him out some coffee! It's got to be freezing out there, and it's going to get worse."

"I have already bring him coffee. He stays outside. You go upstairs and stay in bed."

Any delusion I might have had of independence or maturity dissolved before that cabal glare. I turned and walked sulkily up the stairs.

From my window, I watched as the storm

approached. You could see the lightning stabbing the water miles out to sea. I'd count, one-one-thousand, two-one-thousand, and calculate its distance. Twenty minutes later, the lightning was almost upon us, but the clouds still held back the rain. The air was heavy with ozone and humidity. There was an aura of impending doom hanging over the beach. I left my bed again to go peer down into the street from Julie's window.

In the spill from the streetlight, you could see the swirls of sea mist curling in on themselves, but the rest of the night was so dark that beyond that halo, everything was black. If I squinted, I could barely make out the dim outline of the towncar.

A crack of lightning illuminated the night like a flash. It was a magnificent branch that lit the sky and the street for a full two seconds. A crash of thunder trembled the house seconds later. In the pitch dark that followed, I mentally reviewed the image that I saw during that flash. Like a black and white photograph in my mind, I could clearly see the street, the towncar, the scrabbling brush of the river marsh across the street, everything.

What I couldn't see was Tino in his car. I stared at the blackness where I knew the car was parked, but I couldn't catch a glimpse of movement in the gloom. Minutes passed. My eyes ached from staring at the same spot for so long. Despite the fact that I was waiting for it, when the next flash of lightning lit the street, it startled me.

The car looked very empty.

Why would Tino leave his car with a storm coming in? He would have had to walk. Unless he had someone else pick him up? But why would he leave without letting someone know?

I ran back to my room, grabbed my cell phone, and paged down through the memory until I found Tino's cell number. I pushed 'send' and waited.

It went to voice mail.

I was shrugging my arm into my bathrobe, trying to dial Julie's cell phone at the same time, when a loud boom resonated from outside.

Not a thunderclap. Not a dumpster bang. I now knew the difference. That was a gunshot.

I ran down the stairs like water over rapids, not slowing as I reached the door.

"Ant Bee!" I called out over my shoulder towards Ant Bee's rooms that were off the kitchen. "That was a gunshot! Call the police!"

I didn't wait for her response. I ran out the door into the night.

CHAPTER THIRTY-EIGHT

The town car was unlocked and empty. The keys were in the ignition. A stack of magazines, a couple of paperback novels, two history books that had been checked out of Boston Public Library, three newspapers and a book of crossword puzzles were strewn casually on the passenger seat, but no sign of Tino.

With a slam, I closed the door and walked around the car. The night was cool and misting, the threatened rain had not yet started to fall, so if there was any sign of him around the car, it wouldn't have been washed away yet.

Unfortunately, it was too dark to see anything. I went back into the car, and searched in the glove compartment for a flashlight. No luck. I grabbed the keys and headed for the trunk. Amongst the normal car trunk tackle, I found two gym bags full of clothes (one actually had gym clothes, the other looked more like an emergency overnight bag), a handgun case locked with a sturdy padlock, a Kevlar vest that looked like it was overdue to be honorably retired after repelling one too many shotgun attacks, and an eighteen-inch long police style flashlight, the kind that doubles as a billy club.

I flicked it on. A surprisingly strong beam of light cut the night. The night mist gave it a kind of a light saber effect, extra long. I fought back the urge to swish it through the air and make the Star Wars whirring sounds. I had work to do.

"Tino!" I called out. The fog deadened my voice. There was no echo. It was as if the night had swallowed up all sound.

I flashed the light on the ground as I circled the car again. I really didn't know what I'd expected to find and I found even less. No blatant clues like a note or a bloody footprint were on the pavement and if there was any significance to the smudges in the grit on the asphalt, their meaning was beyond me. Waving the beam in a broader arc, I widened my search.

The tidewater inlet that ran along the other side of the street was separated from the road by a salt marsh. The scrabbly brush was usually undisturbed since the ground quickly dissolved into a shoe-sucking bog that discouraged even the local kids from exploring its secrets.

A darkened fold in the thorny hedge looked a bit off to me, even in the moonless gloom. I waved the beam on that area and I could make out where someone had recently pushed their way through into marsh beyond.

"Tino?" I whispered.

I really did not want to go in there. I looked up and down the street, undecided. Where the police? I should have taken that extra second to make sure that Ant Bee heard me and knew how important it was to call them. I felt the pockets of my robe; I'd left the cell phone upstairs. I stood there waiting for about a minute and a half, bouncing up and down on my toes, as much from nerves as from the need to stay warm. It was after two a.m. and despite the recent gunshot, the street was deathly quiet. Even the swash of the waves sounded muffled. I took a step or two back towards the house, and then froze.

I heard a sound like a low moan from the marsh behind me. Any other night, and I would start imagining marsh ghosts or bog bogies. Tonight however, I had something real to be afraid of.

"Tino?" My voice didn't know whether to whisper or yell, so it cracked instead. "Is that you?"

I heard what I thought was another faint moan and I did something pretty stupid. Grabbing the flashlight, I pushed my way into the marsh.

CHAPTER THIRTY-NINE

Something had been mucking about in the bog. Whoever or whatever it was didn't know much about how to walk through swamps. In the beam from the flashlight, I could see where someone had stepped in to the mud and sank up to their knees, then used their arms to pull themselves out. Whoever it was, they were going to be one muddy mess when they were done. I took a leaping step to land on a small tuft of swampgrass. The roots that bound the mud together provided the only decent footing. I grabbed at a branch to catch my balance and bit my lip as a swatch of thorns cut my hand. I sucked the blood off the heel of my palm, jiggled my fingers to shake off the pain, and then flashed the light to see where the trail led to.

The track was not difficult to follow. If it wasn't for the single-minded direction of the disturbance, I would have thought that someone was just flailing in the mud. Or that it was two people struggling. Yet it was unlikely that a skirmish would be trained in one direction. Panning the area with the light, I slowly followed the trail.

Having spent several dreary adolescent afternoons exploring this marsh, I knew how to walk through it without sinking to my knees, but this didn't mean that I pranced though it like a butterfly. My bare feet were cut and raw from blades of marsh grass and mussel shells. The bottom of my white terry robe was inky black and more than a couple of times, I missed the solid hummock that I was aiming for and slipped into the mud.

The trail led to the river. As it got closer to the water's edge, the tracks started to fade and the ground got soupier. I reached the edge of the scrub and stopped to look around. There weren't enough tufts of vegetation this close to the waterline to navigate. To go any further, I would definitely have to wade thigh deep through mud.

I pointed the flashlight in the direction that the trail would have continued if it hadn't been swallowed up the mire. Nothing moved. Yet as I panned the beam along the water's edge, I noticed a strange lump like the top of an overturned dingy.

Or a human body.

I kept the light fixed on it for several seconds, hoping I could figure out what it was.

I couldn't tell from that distance. I plunged in.

By the time the muck got to be about waist deep, I was doing a modified dog-paddle-crawl. I tossed the flashlight back towards the hummock of marsh grass. I needed both hands to maneuver in the mud. The night was so dark that it wasn't until I was within a couple of feet of the lump that I could see that it really was a body.

It was Tino. It looked like he had crawled out

here and then decided to take a nap. He looked comfortable. If it wasn't for the fact that he was lying face down in icy cold mud.

I waded the last few feet and tugged at his belt to turn him over. I ripped open his shirt and felt for a heartbeat. He was still breathing. His head had been resting on his arm which had kept his nose out of the mud.

He was unconscious and I couldn't tell what injuries he might have. He may have had a concussion or even a gunshot wound, but in the pitch dark, covered with mud, it was impossible to tell.

"Tino!" I hissed at him and shook his shoulders. I was rewarded with the tiniest mumble, but that was it. "Are you okay?"

Lame question. Moving on.

I grabbed him under his arms and tried to pull him back towards the street. I'd made it about five feet before I gave it up. He weighed a ton and I didn't know how badly he'd been hurt. Pulling him like that just might make it worse.

"I'm going for help," I said out loud, more for my benefit than his. "You wait here."

I pulled myself back onto the closest hummock and looked in vain for the flashlight. It was at this moment that the sky decided to open up with all the rain that had been threatening for the past hour.

"Oh that just figures!" I muttered to myself. I stood up and looked back to where Tino lay on his back, the rain pounding on his face. There was nothing else I could do for him except get help. I began the series of calculated steps from one clump of grass to the next.

The scrub rose up on all sides of me as the rain poured down. It's not all that far from the river to the street and I should have reached the pavement by that point, but I got myself turned around and lost my bearings. I stopped by an elder bush, rose up on my toes, and peered into the dark, looking for the streetlight like a beacon.

A shot rang out and a scorching pain seared my right thigh. Someone was shooting at me! Again! My leg gave out under me and I fell to the mud, grabbing at my burning leg.

Four more shots rang out in quick succession; a couple of them hitting the ground close enough to me that I could see the splash of mud as they impacted within feet of me.

That was five shots. Plus the one shot I had heard from the house. Six shots. If I was right and the killer had a six shot .38 revolver, he would have to be reloading now. I leapt to my feet and made a dash into the direction opposite from where I thought the shots were coming from.

I hadn't limped more than a couple of paces before I heard three more shots. Immediately, I tried to drop back to the ground, but my robe got snagged on a branch. I squirmed out of it and fell flat on my face with a splat.

So much for the six shot revolver theory.

I rolled over on my back and watched,

mesmerized, as another flurry of shots was fired into the suspended robe. I lost count. The robe danced and twitched like an epileptic marionette before breaking free and settling to the ground.

That was supposed to be me.

I couldn't move. I lay there motionless, covered with mud, frozen with fear. The rain poured down, the wind howled, thunder rumbled in the distance, but all I could hear was my heart pounding. I may have peed my pants. With all the mud, who could tell?

Something was moving through the brush. A huge dark shape rose up from the murk. It approached the elder tree, stopping to pick up my robe. A distant flash of lightning lit the sky faintly for a moment, enough for me to make out the features of the man as he straightened, his hand clutching the collar.

Tino Scollari.

I must have gasped or made some movement because I could see the silhouette of his head turn in my direction. He dropped the robe and stepped towards me.

I rolled over on to my hands and knees and scuttled across the mud. I could hear the branches snapping and his feet slogging behind me. I crawled on my belly beneath some thorny undergrowth, thinking that the mesh of barbed branches would slow him down.

An iron hand wrapped around my ankle and pulled me back with a sharp jerk. My hands slid out from under me and my chest hit the ground with a breath-robbing thud. As I was dragged backwards, I clawed at the roots and hooked an arm around the slim trunk of a groundsel tree. A short and furious tug of war followed, which I quickly lost; I still hadn't recover my upper body strength from the last gunshot wound.

I felt hands on my hips and I twisted my body around, feet kicking and fingers scratching. The satisfaction of feeling my nails carve gullies into his cheek was short-lived. His knees pressed down on my legs, and my wrists were pinned to the ground. The full weight of his body was on top of me and he leaned his face down to mine.

"Quiet!" he hissed in my ear.

Oh, yeah. And I am *such* an obedient child.

I opened my mouth and took a deep breath, fully prepared to let loose a scream that would hopefully leave him permanently deaf in one ear.

He must have read my intention, because before I could fully catch my breath, his mouth covered mine, robbing me of both my breath and my senses.

I squirmed ferociously. I only wish I could say that my thrashing was ineffective. I could feel something firm hardening against my thighs and I was suddenly aware that what little I was wearing was soaking wet and provided practically no protection against the elements. Any of the elements.

Despite the growing evidence of his lower body, Tino's kiss was anything but romantic. With one swift gulp he sucked the air out of my lungs and literally left me breathless. My nose was pressed flat and I couldn't get any air through it. My struggles quickly exhausted my oxygen supply and I grew dizzy and light-headed. In spite of the adrenalin rush of fear that was still coursing through my body, I was close to passing out. To save my last breath, I froze like a possum.

I lay limply. Tino stayed poised tensely on top of me as if waiting for my next move. When I didn't respond, he pulled his mouth of my mine, his face still hovering inches away.

I gulped air greedily. I hadn't been sure if I ever was going to taste oxygen again.

"Don't move and don't make a sound," he whispered. The tone of his voice did not encourage any debate on the issue. Good enough. I doubted that I would be able to move or speak for a while anyway.

And then with a sudden push off his hands, he rolled off me.

I lay flat on my back, feeling the rain beating against my face, listening anxiously, trying to figure out what he was doing, but I could hear little beyond the sounds of the storm and my own ragged breath. I pushed myself up onto my left elbow and peered into the night.

He was gone.

My right thigh throbbed painfully. I felt it with my fingers. The moisture on that leg was warm. Not a good sign. I was probably bleeding badly. I felt my right shoulder; it was sore from the rough handling, but I didn't think that the stitches had come loose. I pulled myself to my feet and swayed dizzily.

"I told you not to move."

I spun around to face Tino, who re-emerged from the dark behind me. Startled, I took an involuntarily step back and slipped off the hummock. My left foot sank into the mud and my right leg, instinctively moving to balance, gave out on me. I fell and landed on my butt in a bed of thistles.

Before I could begin a scrambling getaway, Tino walked over, reached down and grabbed my flannel nightie below my neck. With one firm yank, he pulled me up, setting me roughly on my feet.

"I can't be sure, but I think he's gone." Tino still held me by the collar of my shirt as he peered in the gloom.

"Who?" I asked stupidly.

"The shooter." Tino answered, his eyes and ears still focused on the surrounding marsh.

I glanced down to the shoulder holster that peeked out from under his open jacket.

"Your gun's missing," I said.

"I know. First thing I looked for when I woke up. You don't happen to know where it is, do you?"

I shook my head. "Woke up?"

He looked down at me, his eyes hard. "And you wouldn't know how I ended up out by the river?"

"I was going to ask you the same thing. I heard

a gunshot and came out to investigate. I tracked you through the marsh and found you there, passed out. I was heading back for help when someone started shooting at me."

His hand released my shirt. I reached down to straighten it, looking to make sure that I was at least partially clothed, when I felt a hand grab a fistful of my hair above the nape. I gasped as he tugged back my head.

"You hear a gunshot outside so you go wandering out into the night, alone and unarmed?" Tino shook his fist and I could feel my brains banging around inside my skull.

"Ow!" I twisted my head free and pushed away from him, but lost my balance and my legs started to fold under me again.

Tino's arm grabbed me around my waist, holding me up.

"What's wrong with you?"

"I got shot in the leg."

"What?" His other arm reached under my knees and he lifted me off my feet. He turned and set me down onto a thorny hummock.

"Ow!" I whined.

"Where does it hurt?" he asked as he took off his jacket.

"My butt! I've got thistles in my butt!"

"Which leg has the bullet wound?" He asked impatiently.

"The one that's bleeding!" I snapped back.

"This one?" He ran his hand over my left leg.

"Or this one?"

I gasped and twisted as his hand came down on the wound.

"That one." He answered his own question, a smug smile in his voice.

Quickly and not gently he wrapped the sleeve of his jacket around the top of my right thigh and pulled it tight. I don't know how he secured it. Before I could even reach down and to feel his makeshift tourniquet, he lifted me in his arms and started wading in the direction which I presumed he thought the street was in.

The rain had let up a bit and the night was not that cold, but I was shivering uncontrollably. He may or may not be a homicidal stalker, but he was warm and I pressed myself against his chest, grateful for that warmth.

Tino's sense of direction was better than mine because in a few minutes we stood on the edge of the marsh, peering into the street. He stopped and checked out the road before emerging from the cover of the foliage.

Nothing moved. You would think that a dozen gun shots would have roused someone, but it was deathly quiet.

"Oh yeah," I muttered to myself. "The Van Hoovens are in Europe." And the Mitchells and the Margolskis wouldn't be down until June. That pretty much left only Ant Bee and she slept with her television on.

Good night for a shootout in Cohasset.

274

Tino opened the back door of the towncar and laid me on the back seat. The cab light flicked on and he checked my leg clinically, and then glanced up at my face.

"You look like hell." He made it sound like a compliment.

"You're looking quite G.Q. yourself." He was a mud-encrusted mess, but it looked good on him. His shirt was pasted to his chest and I could make out every cut of his abs. I'm sure I was a disaster. Why is it that guys can get coated with filth and still look good?

He reached into the front seat and stopped.

"Where are my car keys?" he asked

"Check the trunk lock. I was looking for a flashlight."

He disappeared only to return a moment later with an armload of stuff. He dropped a couple of layers of gym clothes on my chest and then started wrapping my leg with some bandages.

"Not bad," he said. "It just a flesh wound, but you've lost a lot of blood and you're in shock."

His fingers felt hot against my thighs as he carefully loosened the tourniquet. I fidgeted nervously.

"I need a shower. I need a change of clothes. I need to pull these thistles out of my butt."

"You need to stay warm and you need to get to the hospital. I'll take you to the emergency room."

Oh, no. Not another emergency room. I squirmed in an effort to get out of the car.

"No you don't." Tino pushed me back down onto the seat.

"Oooh." I landed hard on my behind. I turned onto my left side and my hand groped blindly on my butt as I tried to find the thistles.

"Oh, for god sakes." Tino sounded aggravated. "I'll do it."

I bit my lip as I felt Tino's hands run lightly up my thigh, the tips of his fingers gliding over the wet flannel. He would pause when he found a snag and then gently pull out the barb, massaging the spot with his thumb before moving on.

I'm absolutely positive that it was just the symptoms of trauma and blood loss, but I really thought my entire body was going to implode.

He finished his explorations on that cheek, sliding his palm down slowly and soothingly from waist to knee and then up again in a final pass before softly patting my butt.

"Okay, that one's done. Roll over so I can get the other."

His voice was impassive but unusually breathless. I turned my head to look closely at his face.

"You're enjoying this, aren't you?" I asked.

"Joey," he said as he stoically lifted my hips and rolled me onto my stomach, "I should get the Eagle Scout badge for self-control. I'm just amazed that I haven't come in my pants yet."

My eyes widened as I glanced down at said pants. He wasn't joking. I made a move to escape, but his hands tightened on my hips and held me in place.

"Don't worry. I'll behave myself."

Damn.

"You know you said that out loud."

I buried my face into the vinyl seat, bit my lip, and let him get back to the task at hand.

CHAPTER FORTY

I watched the dawn arrive from a curtained cubicle in the Weymouth General Hospital. It had been a bit like old-home week, the staff all remembered me from my last bullet wound. Nurse Scratchit fawned all over me. It was as if getting shot twice in two weeks gave me some kind of pseudo-celebrity status.

I hadn't seen Tino in the last couple of hours. When we first arrived, he had me admitted. A doctor quickly looked at the bandage, but didn't take it off. After the doctor disappeared, a Cohasset policeman arrived and questioned us.

About an hour later, McBeige showed up with his trenchcoat draped over his arm. I guess he didn't want it to get it wet in the rain. I was feeling a little wiped out, so I let Tino do most of the talking, just adding my two cents here and there. Finally, they came to put me into an examination room and Tino left with McBeige.

Nurse Scratchit was playing bulldog when McBeige came back an hour or so later. As she left, her glare threatened all kinds of dire consequences if I suffered a relapse.

I gave McBeige my version of what happened in

the marsh and then he asked me to repeat it all again because his stupid little tape recorder hadn't been working. It was well after seven o'clock in the morning before we were done.

Tino hadn't reappeared, there was no answer at Julie's apartment or her cell phone and the phone at the house went straight to the message machine. I wanted to go home. I needed a shower. I needed real clothes. I needed to sleep in my own bed.

"Do you know where Tino got to?" I asked McBeige as he was leaving.

He stopped in the doorway and shot me a look which I couldn't understand, never mind describe.

"He's under arrest."

"For what?" My voice had a sharper edge than I intended, but shock will do that to you.

"Attempted murder, for starters." McBeige watched me intently.

"Of who?"

"You." He turned and walked back into the room, shutting the door behind him. "Our crime scene team combed the site this morning. We found Scollari's Glock in the grass, recently fired, the magazine was empty. We recovered two of the bullets and they're a match. His prints are the only prints on the gun and there is no evidence of anyone else but the two of you at the crime scene. He tested positive for gunpowder residue on his hands and the scratches on his face match up to the tissue samples taken from under your nails."

"Wow, you guys move fast."

It was the first thing that came into my head. I was stalling. I needed time to think. Had I really been so blinded by the physical attraction that I misread everything? And yet something was not right.

"The D.A.'s motivated on this one. He doesn't want to let Scollari get away with it again."

"Again?"

"Hatteras hasn't forgotten the Mavros murder, eight years ago."

My mind jumped back to last night. "If Tino was trying to kill me, he could have strangled me when he found me in the marsh."

"We don't know why he didn't. We're not even fully certain what his motive is. It might be that he planned to kill you, and then changed his mind. Whatever his reason, we're not giving him another chance. Hatteras wants him held without bail."

It wasn't making sense. Tino wasn't stupid. He wouldn't use his own gun and then toss it away where it could be found. I'll admit that when he first found me in the marsh, I thought he might be the killer, but his actions afterwards made me change my mind.

Unless he's schizophrenic. That would explain trying to kill me one minute and then save me the next. It would also explain how he can be coming on to two sisters at the same time.

Let's not go there right now.

"Do you need a ride home? I can send a squad car to drop you."

I looked up to see McBeige's eyes on me.

"No thanks. My sister's on her way." I lied.

"I'll type up your statement and come by this evening so that you can sign it."

When I didn't respond, he nodded a silent goodbye and left.

I was still in a shocked funk when Nurse Scratchit walked back in and started fussing with the sheets.

"You're all set now." Her voice was a gravely bark. "We had your information on file from your last visit, so you can leave as soon as your ride shows up."

"Okay, thanks." My eyes were fixed blindly on the bed stand and my voice was as blank as my eyes.

I didn't want to believe it could be Tino, but did that mean he didn't do it?

Sometimes our hearts can see truths that our minds are blind to.

Venerable words of wisdom or the ravings of a homicidal schizophrenic?

My head hurt.

Nurse Scratchit left, leaving behind a small damp stack of clothes. I picked up my muddied and ripped pajamas off the pile and dropped them into the trash barrel. They were too far gone to be saved. The rest of the clothes were Tino's gym clothes. I pulled on his tee shirt and sweat pants. They swam on me but at least I was out of the paper hospital gown that had kept me hiding under the covers for the last few hours. Tino's jacket was there too. I shrugged it on. It was damp and bloodstained and smelled of Tino.

It also had his car keys in the pocket.

CHAPTER FORTY-ONE

If we're making a list of stupid things not to do, we can add driving oneself home from the hospital after a bullet wound.

I told the guy at the checkout desk that my ride was outside. I waved merrily to a total stranger who returned the greeting, very confused. When he reached for the phone to arrange for a wheelchair to take me the last twenty feet out to the curb, I slipped out the door.

It took me more than a few minutes to find Tino's car in the parking garage. He still had over half a tank of gas in it. I slid the driver's seat up so that I could reach the pedals, turned on the engine, then rested my forehead against the steering wheel as the car warmed up.

Maybe sitting in the same seat where Tino had been would inspire me to figure out what the hell happened last night.

That first gunshot that drew me out of the house, who or what had he been shooting at? And was he faking being unconscious in the marsh? If it was to draw me out, why wouldn't he kill me then? I couldn't recall if the gun was in his shoulder holster when I turned him over and I knew that a

Glock would still be able to fire if it got damp or muddy. But why let me walk away and then shoot at me from a distance?

I looked around at the car, hoping for a clue. It didn't look like the police had been through it yet. Maybe they didn't know where Tino had parked it. I might be messing with evidence, but since no one told me not to, I wasn't stopping now.

I went through the stack of books and papers that had been pushed to the floor on the passenger's side. I flipped through the leaves of the books. A blank note card acted as a book mark on one of the books, but beyond that, nothing. The books had been checked out of the Boston Public Library three days ago. Both of yesterday's papers were there, the Herald and the Globe. The crossword in the Herald was done, the Globe's just started. He did them in ink with many crossovers. The magazines didn't look as if they'd even been opened yet.

Nothing unusual on the seat, over the visor or in the glove compartment. The radio, CB and the police scanner, were all as I remembered them. I didn't have a pencil, so I couldn't pencil-etch the visor notepad to see what he had written recently. I'd do that when I got home.

The back seat had mud, blood and a few stray remnants of Tino's gym clothes, but nothing else.

And yet there was something wrong, something out of sync, but I couldn't put my finger on it.

It was as I was about to put the car into gear and back out that I realized that the clue I was looking for wasn't something that was in the car.

It was something that wasn't.

I stared at the wall of the parking garage, my mind flicking through all the facts that I knew, all the evidence that I'd read, every element that I thought I should consider.

The engine was just heating up but I felt chilled to the bone. Like a perfect break on a billiard table, one at a time the balls rolled into their pockets, the facts clicked into place.

"That's ridiculous!" I muttered to myself. "Absurd."

And yet, the more I thought about it, the clearer it got. I shivered from more than the cold, hugging the damp clothes closer to my skin.

I grabbed the keys and walked around to the trunk. Tino's overnight bag was still there. I pulled on a few more layers of clothes, shut the trunk, and headed back for the driver's seat. There is a time to hide and a time to attack. A time to retreat and a time to wait.

I knew what time it was.

CHAPTER FORTY-TWO

I left the car in the same spot Tino had parked in the night before. The police line tape was still draped along the edge of the marsh. I stood at the curb and stared in.

It looked like a high school football team had been skirmishing in the mud. The brush was trampled and clumps of dirt spread into the street showing where the police crews had stomped the worst of the muck off their boots as they left.

If the marsh held any more secrets about last night, I certainly wasn't going to be the one to go in there in find them. I turned and looked at the house.

I needed a shower. I needed dry clothes. I needed to sleep. But there were a few other things I had to do first. I crossed the street and went into the house.

Ant Bee's car was in the garage, next to my Lexus. I walked into the kitchen, not announcing myself as I usually do. I could hear Ant Bee futzing around in her room. The door was open; I walked over and stood in the doorway.

She was folding her laundry. I could tell by the way she kept her face pointed away that she knew that I was there, but she was determined not to acknowledge my invasion of her demesnes.

I waited. She finished folding her clothes and started to pull the sheets off her bed, a clean stack of linen still sitting in the hamper. As she laid out the bottom sheet, she finally met my eye. She didn't speak, she just raised one eyebrow.

"Why?" It was only question I really wanted to have answered.

"Vy, vat?" She was not going to make this easy.

"You said you brought coffee to Tino last night, but there was no coffee cup in his car."

"Pffft." Hungarian for *so what?*

"You're possibly the only person who knew for a fact that I was going over to Phillip's the night Lucy Rudd was shot. And one of the few who would have guessed I would be heading down to the breakwater when I slipped out to take a walk that night."

With a practiced wave of the bedspread, Ant Bee finished making her bed. It was a marvel of military precision, not a single wrinkle. And still she said nothing.

"Last night, you brought out drugged coffee to Tino. That's why you didn't want me to go out and check on him. Did you have help or did you really drag him all the way to river yourself?"

She finally spoke.

"Hungarian women are much stronger than you pansy Americans." Her voice was cool, emotionless, as if she were answering an obvious math problem.

"You laid him face down in the mud, thinking he'd drown. Then you put his own gun in his hand and fired it. That would not only leave the gunshot residue on him, but it would also pull me out of the house and get me into the marsh. You could then shoot me with Tino's gun, leave it in the weeds, and in the morning it would look like a drugged out Tino had shot me and then got himself turned around in the marsh, accidentally drowning."

"Clever," she said. I don't know if she was congratulating herself for her plan, or me, for figuring it out. Funny thing, I wasn't in the mood to be flattered.

"The only question I have is, why?"

Seconds turned into minutes and neither of us spoke. I needed the answer. Finally, Ant Bee cocked her head to one side as if listening to something that only she could hear. Then, with what I can only describe as a cheerful chuckle, she spoke.

"You are *sárkány*. The evil seed. You steal from your sister. I watch while you take all her father's love. I tell her that you are evil, but she laughs and says, no, she does not mind that you are the favorite daughter. But I know she lies. You take her inheritance and give her only drips and draps of what is rightfully hers. And when she meets a man she likes, you steal that too. You are *sárkány*. It is not a surprise that there is one that tries to kill you. It is only a surprise that no one has done it before."

I think I liked Ant Bee better when she was shooting at me.

I could feel my legs trembling and I folded my arms across my chest, my fingernails digging into my elbows as if to keep myself from flying into shreds.

"No," I heard myself say as if from a place far away. "That's not right."

Ant Bee had turned to pull a stack of clothes from one of her dresser drawers, but she looked up as I spoke and narrowed her eyes.

"If you were that concerned with Julie's feelings, you wouldn't have tried to kill Scollari."

"He was her boyfriend and then he starts sniffing around you like a *kutya*. He doesn't deserve my princess."

Wow. I always knew she like Julie better, but, boy, did I underestimate by how much.

And yet, it still didn't sound right.

"No." I said again, shaking my head. "This *is* about Scollari, but it's not about what's best for Julie. For years, Julie's been going around promising to just about everyone that when she comes into her inheritance, she'll be giving away big chunks of money. When Dad died, you thought your chance had come, but she didn't hold the purse strings, I did, so you waited. But when Julie got involved with Tino, you were worried that he wasn't going to be a soft touch like Julie. You panicked. You couldn't wait for the trust to wrap up, so you decided to expedite things by killing me."

It sounded good to me, but the look on Ant

Bee's face was mocking. She was almost laughing at me.

"You were always a stupid child." She spat the words at me. "A stupid, selfish, arrogant child. And as usual, you are wrong."

I wasn't going to get any more out of her. I headed out the door.

"Dead wrong," she muttered.

I turned back to see Ant Bee holding a revolver. You would think that with the week I'd been having, I would be used to having a gun pointed at me, but my heart stopped dead for a second and then started up again, rattling like a machine gun.

Ant Bee was done talking. I saw her finger close on the trigger. I spun around and dived for the door and was almost there when I heard the double click of a hammer cocking and a cylinder rolling, but no gunshot followed. The sound repeated two more times. I turned back, primal fear quickly changing to raging anger as I realized the gun was either empty or misfiring.

"Oh, *fakanal*," she muttered.

I took an angry step back into the room when something hit me in the chest with the force of a freight train. I would later swear the sound of the gunshot happened after I felt the impact. My feet left the ground and I flew backward into the kitchen, hitting my head on the island counter.

The room was fading in and out, and out was winning. The last thing I remembered was Ant Bee, walking toward me from her bedroom, the gun in one hand, a suitcase in the other.

CHAPTER FORTY-THREE

Nurse Scratchit was euphoric.

"Three gunshots wounds in two weeks." I could hear her announcing to complete strangers in the hallway. "That's a record for the hospital. Possibly all of New England."

"Technically," I yelled from my bed, "it's not a gunshot wound."

Julie and Tino were sitting next to the bed. Julie was grinning. Tino was not amused.

"Feels just like a kick in the chest, doesn't it?" asked Julie.

"More like getting flattened by a Mini-Cooper." My voice was a little breathy because I could only take small short gulps of air. "Did *you* break any ribs when you got shot?"

"No, but I was a little more than five feet away from the gun when it went off. And that vest you snagged from Tino's trunk was pretty ratty."

"When you two are done comparing war wounds, I have a question." Tino's voice was icy cold.

Julie and I turned to Tino.

"What the hell were you thinking of?" Tino bellowed. The vein in his neck pulsed. "A Kevlar vest is only effective if you're shot in the chest! What if she had shot you in the head? If Julie hadn't been pulling into the driveway when the first shot went off, she probably would have!"

"Well, I didn't think she was actually going to shoot me."

Tino slapped his forehead.

"You do that a lot, you know." I said. "You should be careful. You might cause brain damage."

Julie's giggle was cut short by Tino's glare.

"I think brain damage is a prerequisite to working with you two." He pulled his hand off his brow and glared at me. "She'd already shot you twice, and she killed Lucy Rudd, thinking it was you. Whatever made you think she wouldn't shoot at you again?"

"Well, I didn't know for a fact that it was Ant Bee. I knew she had the opportunity. I was guessing on the motive. So I figured the only thing left was the confession. How else was I going to get it if I didn't ask her?"

"What," Tino asked slowly, "are you babbling about?"

I sighed and shook my head.

"M.O.C." I said, as if explaining it to a three year old.

"M.O.C." he echoed.

"Motive. Opportunity. Confession." I said smugly.

"Where did you hear that hogwash?"

"Um, Detective McBeige. In the police station." I

was quickly losing my smugness.

"With the candlestick!" added Julie.

Tino went back to striking himself on the forehead.

"Joey," he said wearily, "motive, opportunity and even confessions are the least conclusive elements of an investigation. Evidence is what you need to look for."

"Oh."

"Evidence. The fact that Ant Bee told you that she had given me coffee, but that the coffee cup had disappeared from the car... that is an important piece of evidence. If you had called McBe---, McAdams, and told him that, he would have gone with you to the house, you wouldn't have gotten shot again, and Ant Bee would be in custody."

"Oh," I said again. Tino could be such a buzz kill. "Have they found her yet?"

"Not yet." It was Julie that answered. "They found her Saab parked at Logan Airport, but the police can't find any record of her getting on a plane."

"That's because Bertuska Czigany, didn't get on a plane," said Detective McBeige.

"Cripe on a bike!" I clutched my chest as the heart monitor by the side of my bed started to blip spastically. "How do you do that?"

McBeige had appeared in the room, at least five feet inside the door. No one had seen him come in. He wore his trench coat, (why not? it was a warm and sunny afternoon) and instead of the notorious tape recorder, he held a thick file in his hand. He opened it and started reading from one of the pages.

"At eight eighteen this morning, Helga Mueller boarded a plane bound for Mexico City using a German passport. Mexico Immigration does not show her clearing Customs. At two thirty two pm, local time, records show a Melina Rigofsky, a citizen of Slovakia, leaving from a small airport outside Mexico City on a commuter plane headed for Belize. We have contacted the Belize authorities and they will be meeting the plane when it lands."

"Wow." Julie's voice was hushed with awe. "Way to go, Ant Bee."

I slapped Julie's arm and she shrugged an apology, but I had to admit, it was an impressive escape.

"She had two false passports?" Tino's eyes narrowed. "Where did an immigrant housekeeper get the money and the connections to engineer a getaway like that?"

"Well, that's where it gets interesting." McBeige grinned like a cat.

"Oh, good," I whispered loudly to Julie, "'cause my life has been so monotonous lately."

McBeige chose to ignore me. "There is no such person as Bertuska Czigany."

He paused for effect.

Note to self: Next time I get shot, bring along the portable keyboard so that I can play dramatic organ chords on cue.

"Her real name is Sibyl Simonyl Ravuski."

"That sounds more Russian than Hungarian," said Julie.

"She was born in Hungary and married three times. All three of her husbands were connected to the Russian Mafia."

"She was a Russian Mafia Doña?" Julie seemed inappropriately impressed by that.

"Actually," McBeige continued, "she was an assassin known on three continents as *űrhajósnő*, the space witch."

"Ant Bee was a Russian Mafia hitwoman?" Julie asked, not even trying to hide her delight.

"She was until she was caught and indicted by the Soviet police in the early eighties. She was given a choice: either the death penalty or she could defect to the United States and act as a deep undercover agent, to be called up as needed."

"Ant Bee was a Russian Mafia hitwoman turned KGB mole?" Julie was almost jumping up and down on her chair in glee.

"I'm afraid so." McBeige was apologetic.

"That is so *cool!*" She collapsed back onto her chair, exhausted from ecstasy.

McBeige looked more than a little taken aback.

"What did you expect?" I said, cradling my forehead in my hands. "Did you think she'd be upset?"

McBeige retreated to the safety of his notes. "When the Soviet Union collapsed in the eighties so did the KGB. Any moles still in this country were left high and dry. Some quietly slipped back into

Russia, but most just stayed where they were, living out their covers, waiting for the KGB to resurrect itself. Or not. The Soviet records were pretty well destroyed so neither the Russian Government nor the U.S. Government really know how many there are still here. And since their lives here are, for the most part, better than what they could expect back home, most have stayed put."

"How do you know so much about, um, Ant Bee?" Tino wasn't even going to try to pronounce any of her names.

"Well, considering her past, she's pretty high profile. The CIA knew she'd been planted, but was never able to trace her. She just never showed up on their radar."

"What about her mother?" asked Julie. She had calmed down enough to be relatively coherent.

"Her mother?" asked Tino.

"Yeah," Julie said soberly. "Her mother has a congenital heart defect and needs corrective surgery. I was going to ask you about that. She didn't want me to bother, but I figure that there are aid organizations that could help people like that."

I looked at Tino and Tino looked at me. I turned back to Julie.

"Julie. Did you give Ant Bee money for her mother?"

Julie nodded guiltily.

"How much?"

"I don't know. A little bit here, a little bit there. She's always been sending money back to Hungary for her mother. But a month or two ago, her mother got really sick and needed the operation so..." Julie's voice trailed off lamely.

"Julie?" Tino's attitude was abrupt and searching. "Did you tell Ant Bee that you were going to ask me to find her mother?"

I could tell by the way that Julie looked around that she was feeling guilty about her answer, but didn't know why. Yet.

"Yeah," she nodded slowly, "she didn't want me to make a fuss, but..."

Her voice faded off. Tino and McBeige exchanged glances.

"Well that would do it," said McBeige.

"Do what?" asked Julie.

Tino answered. "With the connections I've got with the Feds and the CIA, if I had started searching for Bet..., Bertru..., for Ant Bee's mother, it probably wouldn't have taken me long to discover that she didn't exist."

"And that would have been all the attention that the CIA would have needed in order to identify her," added McBeige.

"Yes, but..." I needed to ask the million dollar question. "Why kill me?"

"To engineer the kind of escape that *Bertuska Czigany* just executed..." McBeige shot a smirk at Tino, "she would have had this all planned out months in advance, if not years. But why she waited this long is the question."

"Julie," I asked, "how much money did you tell

Ant Bee that you would give her?"

"Two." Julie mumbled, looking down at her feet.

"Two dollars?" asked McBeige.

Julie shook her head.

"Two thousand dollars?" asked Tino.

Again, Julie shook her head.

I sighed. They did not know my sister.

"Two hundred thousand dollars," I said, not the least bit surprised.

Julie nodded guiltily.

We observed a moment of silence as the gentlemen dealt with their shock. Not me. I'd been coping with this for years.

"Well, that would be worth waiting around for," McBeige said tactfully.

Nurse Scratchit entered at this point and rousted my guests; the doctor was coming by in a few minutes to check me out before letting me go home.

"Do you mind if I talk to my sister for a minute?" I asked.

Julie was halfway out the door, but stopped and waited. Nurse Scratchit folded her arms and looked forbidding. Yeah, she'd have made a great nun.

"It's important," I added.

Nurse Scratchit broke down and gave me a smile and a maternal pat. After all, I was the one who brought a level of notoriety to the Weymouth General Hospital such as they had never enjoyed before. With a parting warning glare to Julie, she left, closing the door behind her.

"Wow, she'd have made a great nun!" Julie grinned.

"Yeah, I know."

"She's even got the facial hair and everything!"

I smiled, but I was already thinking ahead to what I was going to say. Julie, picking up on my mood, sat down on the edge of the bed and waited.

I didn't know how to start, so I just took a deep breath and plunged in.

"Ant Bee and I had one of our more pleasant chats this morning."

"Before or after she started shooting."

"Um, that would be, before."

"Right."

"She-called-me-the-evil-seed-and-said-that-I-stole-Dad-from-you." I said that all in one breath. I think that it could technically be considered as being all one word.

Julie dropped her eyes to the hands clenched in her lap. I watched her warily as her shoulders shook. When she looked up, I saw she her eyes streaming with tears.

"Don't laugh at me!" I snapped. "I'm serious!"

"I'm sorry." She hiccupped as she wiped her eyes. "It's just that you're so funny!"

"I'm not trying to be funny! So knock it off!"

After a moment of biting her lip, Julie calmed back down.

"Um, Jo, you may have missed this, but Ant Bee didn't like you."

I snorted. "Really? She hid it so well."

"Dad didn't love me less than he loved you... he just loved me different. Ant Bee could never see that. You and Dad were so much alike. You spoke the same language, thought the same way. When you guys talked business, you wouldn't even have to finish your sentences, you were both so much on the same page.

"You two would jump from tangent to tangent, I couldn't even begin to follow what you were talking about. It was like trying to watch T.V. with someone sitting on the remote.

"But when Dad and I talked, it was about stuff like boys and school... and Mama."

I looked up sharply at that. Dad had rarely mentioned Mama to me.

"I don't have many memories of Mama," Julie continued, looking at me but not seeing me at all, "but Dad said that I reminded him of her. He used to tell me stories of the things that she would say or do. The crazy stunts she would pull when they were dating and even after she had us. She was a little wacko."

With a shrug, Julie returned from wherever she and her memories had been visiting.

"You and Dad had the business thing in common, but me and Dad, we had Mama."

Suddenly, I felt shortchanged. *I* wanted to talk to Dad about Mama, but I never had.

And now I never would.

"We are so different, Jo," Julie said with a small

smile. "The fact that Dad loved us differently isn't a big deal."

I felt like a penny, spinning on a table. In a moment, I was going to spin lower and land. Heads: I would feel cheated. Tails: I'd feel relieved.

Mentally, I scooped up the coin and shoved it into an emotional pocket. I'd have to deal with that later, Julie was changing the subject.

"So, what's the deal with you and Tino?" Julie's voice was much too nonchalant.

Oh, God. Here it comes.

"Tino and I?" I am so not good at sounding innocent when I'm feeling guilty.

"Is it 'Tino and I' or is it 'Tino and me'?"

And at a time like this, she looking for grammatical clarity.

"It's Tino and you." Boy, did it hurt to say that.

She thought about that one for a moment.

"That doesn't help."

"I've decided to give him up." There. I've said it.

"Who?"

"Tino."

"Give him up to what?" she asked.

"You know."

"You haven't even started dating yet and you're already dumping him?"

"I can't date him," I said miserably.

"Why not?"

"Cause you are!"

"I am?"

"Of course you are!" I was stopped by the expression on her face. "Aren't you?"

"No!"

"But you said he was the greatest guy you ever met!"

"He is. But we're not dating. I was kind of hoping that if you and he hit it off, you'd dump Phillip." She whispered, as if it were a secret, "I really don't like Phillip."

My sister is insane. My entire world was spinning upside down and only one fact remained clear: my sister is insane.

"So this whole detective thing has just been a ploy to set us up?"

"Well, no. I do think this is what I want to do. I think I can be good at it. And Tino told me that a lot of his cases involve corporate stuff and I figured that you could be good at that."

At that moment, I was not going to deal with her delusions that I had any intention of ever becoming a private detective.

"But you've been having dinner with him almost every night," I said, returning to the big problem.

"I like spaghetti."

"You like spaghetti? That's it?"

"Well no. The meatballs are good too."

I felt like a balloon after it's sailed around the room and is now sitting in a deflated heap in the corner.

"I have to run," Julie said with a very self-satisfied smile. "I'll ask Tino to drive you home."

She was gone before I could respond.

Nurse Scratchit and the doctor came in. I answered their questions mechanically; my mind was outside in the hall where I could see Tino waiting, his back towards the door, watching the hospital traffic like a Doberman on duty. My eyes wandered down to his jeans and I found myself wondering how he would look naked.

Sister Benignus would kill me. I am so going to burn in hell.